D1632724

Life... On A High

Nick Spalding is back... and this time he's airborne!

By popular demand (and because those counselling sessions won't pay for themselves) Nick returns in the sequel to Life... With No Breaks, with a new collection of anecdotes, stories and asides.

This time he's writing at 40,000 feet... and what better way is there to kill forty eight hours on a round trip to Australia than holding another conversation with *you*?

Sit back - don't worry, we're in Business Class so the seats are comfortable - put your feet up, and laugh out loud as Nick wends his merry way through a plethora of subjects, including age, hobbies, crime, dating the wrong women and pretending to be a banana (among many other things).

After you've read Life... On A High, you may never look at the rest of the world the same way again!

By Nick Spalding

Coronet Books

Love... From Both Sides
Love... And Sleepless Nights

Racket Publishing

Life... With No Breaks
Life... On A High
The Cornerstone

Life... On A High

Nick Spalding

Racket Publishing

Chapters

The Flight to Australia

The Flight to the UK

The Flight to Australia

Well, well, well.

Here we are again…

Actually, that's massively inaccurate, as the last time we crossed paths it was in my comfy, warm study back at home.

And now?

We're just levelling out at about 40,000 feet, having had a relatively smooth take off from Heathrow.

Yes indeed, it's your old pal Nickle-Pickle, back by popular demand and here to regale you with even more embarrassing anecdotes and half-arsed observations about the wonderful world we live in.

I'm currently flying high above said wonderful world in a long metal tube with wings, being propelled along by a scientific phenomenon I've never entirely understood. I do know it's got something to do with air pressure, and a complicated principle invented by an Italian bloke called Bernoulli.

I though he sold pizzas, but what the hell do I know?

Anyway, after what feels like a lifetime since knocking out Life… With No Breaks, I'm once again sat at the keyboard, trying my hardest to think of something interesting to write.

I must be mental.

To be honest, this is all *your* fault.

It was *very* insensitive of you to like Life… With No Breaks and buy all those copies of it, because now I *have* to write a sequel.

As we all know, sequels are never as good:

The Matrix Reloaded. Batman and Robin. Saw's 2 through 7. Return Of The Killer Tomatoes. Fletch Lives. All the Star Wars prequels.

See what I mean?

Terrible!

There's always a weight of expectation that comes packaged with sequels.

There will be inevitable comparisons to the original – and nine times out of ten the audience will think the second effort isn't as good and doesn't come up to scratch.

Chances are they'll also believe it was only written for the money. I will cheerfully admit that in this assessment of *my* second book, they would be absolutely right.

Comparisons with what has gone before are never a good thing.

I can only wonder how George Lazenby felt stepping into Sean Connery's shoes to play James Bond, or Irvin Kershner when he took over from George Lucas directing the sequel to Star Wars. I'm sure they put a brave face on it, but it must have been pretty bloody terrifying.

…not that I'm comparing my grotty little books to two of the most successful film franchises in history, you understand. My ego hasn't inflated *that* much.

I'm tempted to say that writing a sequel is even more difficult when the person you're being compared to is *you*.

How psychologically damaging is that?

I went back and read LWNB (yes, it's popular enough now justify its own acronym… woo hoo!) for the first time in months and it transpires it's pretty good. The reviews left by the lovely people who bought it seem to agree - for the most part, anyway.

Aaargh!

What an utter *bastard* me from the past is, for writing something deserving of a high rating.

How the hell am I supposed to compete with that?

In what will probably turn out to be a vain and failed attempt to recreate the magic of the first book, I've come up with another narrative device to hang stories, anecdotes and musings around.

I couldn't do the whole 'writing a book in one sitting' thing again. I had to spend £250 on a course of extensive massage therapy just so I could get the feeling back in my arse and walk in a straight line.

The chair I sat in has long since given up the ghost and the ceiling needed repainting twice to cover up the nicotine stains.

Nevertheless, the idea for another way to write a 'Life…' book was presented to me and after much deliberation I decided to have a crack at it.

Sequels always try to go one better than the original, but invariably fall short. This is called *Die Harder* syndrome.

So…

This time round we're on a plane!

I liked the narrative device of writing a book in a confined period of time and if there's ever an occasion when you're confined *for* an extended period of time, it's on a long haul flight.

This particular plane is heading for sunny Australia.

Not on *holiday* to Australia, sadly.

This is a work trip that'll see me gallivanting around lots of air conditioned offices in New South Wales, wishing I was outside on a beach somewhere having fun. It doesn't matter how lovely the weather is if you're stuck indoors watching the seventh PowerPoint presentation in a row that day.

Still, it's a twenty four hour flight there and a twenty four hour flight back - more than enough time for me to crank out another 50,000 words to entertain you - until that Discovery documentary about Hitler going on in the corner of the room gets really interesting and you put me down for the rest of the evening.

I'm retaining the time checks as they made good chapter breaks last time out, but you'll see I'm also including geographical reference points this time, to keep you abreast of our progress towards the Antipodes.

Exciting, isn't it?

The TV in front of me has got one of those jazzy maps showing a little graphic of the plane, so I can chart exactly where I am in the world. I was planning on giving you the distance in miles and latitude & longitude figures, but this is supposed to be a light hearted comedy book and not a horrifically dull cartography manual, so I wisely thought better of it.

Once again, I'm doing this whole thing by the seat of my pants.

I haven't planned what I'm going to write, or how long I'll keep going before this plane touches down back at Heathrow. I will no doubt meander through any topic, memory or opinion that floats through my brain, hoping to turn my thoughts into an entertaining read for you - my friend and confidante in this (second) great undertaking.

I may start on one subject, only to veer off on an annoying tangent into another story entirely. I apologise in advance for this. I'm afraid you have to take the rough with the smooth with this kind of book. The downs with the ups, as it were... the frowns with the laughs. The cowpats with the golden nuggets.

Let's just hope the balance is more in favour of the latter as we wend our way through the next several thousand words, eh?

I am approaching things with a bit more confidence this time, having already written a book like this.

Like anything in life, the second time is always easier.

…unless you're over seventy and going back for seconds.

...

Oh, alright. I can't lie to you!

Maybe I have done *some* preparation, knowing full well I've got something to live up to. I've got to pull out all the stops if I'm going to come up to the standard set previously, so I decided a little forethought and planning couldn't hurt.

This involved spending an hour last night (with the packing only half done) thinking about what topics to talk about in the pages of this sequel.

I have them scrawled on the back of a used envelope, tacked to the wall in front of me next to the telly screen.

...so when I say I've done *some* preparation, what I actually mean is *very little.*

I'm lazy, I know - I can't help it.

Please try not to judge me.

Here I sit then... in British Airways Club World no less!

Yes, my usually stingy company has sprung for some nice seats for once.

This isn't because they read my fascinating diatribe on flying in the first book and decided to take pity on me, but because we've been quite successful recently – despite the recession - having landed a couple of lucrative contracts.

One of these is to create a mountain of promotional material for a sport fitness empire based in Sydney that's bringing its operation to the UK - hence this flight and the opportunity to crank out another book.

No worries about being cramped, getting dribbled on by a pensioner, or inadvertently molesting one of the seats this time. Club World is *far* classier than that.

I'm sat in relative luxury in a little white booth, feet up and laptop resting on my legs.

...it's now a Hewlett Packard Pavilion 2.1ghz dual core with 3gb of RAM if you're interested ... and you *still* need to get out more.

There's only three other people here with me. It's a night flight, so most sensible folk are at home tucked up in bed.

The cabin is pretty much silent at the moment, except for the low hum of the Rolls Royce engines and the gentle tap-tap of my fingers on the keyboard.

And look!

As if it was meant to be: There's an empty booth opposite that looks perfect for you.

Don't worry, no-one's going to mind you having it, I'm sure.

———

It's just going to waste otherwise.

If you're going to keep me company as I fly across the world, you'll need somewhere nice and comfortable to sit, won't you?

The blanket looks quite snug if you get cold and there's one of those miniature pillows that are never as soft as they look.

Feel free to steal the headphones when we land, I'm sure they won't mind. I'm going to. They look a lot better than the ones that came with my iPod.

Why not take advantage of all the luxury BA have laid on and crank the chair back into its reclined position?

I have to sit more or less upright so I can use the computer, but that doesn't mean you can't revel in the opulence a business class ticket affords.

I'm afraid the choice of snacks isn't down to me this time. We're both victims of the culinary delights BA have on offer, I'm afraid. Happily, we're not in economy class, so it shouldn't taste like cardboard and look like cat sick, but I can't promise anything more than that. At least it's free though, eh?

I'm sure the coffee will be of a higher standard than mine. I very much doubt it's been standing at room temperature in a broken thermos flask for several hours.

If you do get peckish before the meals arrive, let me know and I'll go and steal some peanuts from the galley. It'll give me a good excuse to chat up the rather attractive stewardess who's floating about the cabin ensuring our needs are met.

…oh dear, that's naughty of me. I'm not a single man anymore, so really shouldn't be thinking of such things. I can't help it, though. The blouse she's wearing is *very* tight.

Chances are I'll broach the story of how I met my latest love interest at some point in the next few chapters, so watch this space…

You won't have to worry about any choking cigarette smoke as we talk, as sparking up isn't allowed on the big tin birds these days.

I quit about a year ago anyway - much to everyone's surprise, including mine.

I'll tell you about that as well, because I'm quite proud of the achievement, and have to make an effort to balance all the dreadful things I do with something positive now and again – mainly to avoid a swift plummet into gormless self pity that'll be no fun for anyone.

So there you have it my friend, the stage is once again set and we can now wade into the book proper, safe in the knowledge that the pesky prologue is well and truly out of the way.

We're going to have fun, you and I… and talk the flight away…

If you're very observant, you'll notice that through the course of this book my hourly output will be somewhat slower than previous. This is because I have forty eight hours of total writing time and the luxury of pacing myself a bit.

You really don't want me spewing out two thousand words an hour anyway, because that gets us to a length of nearly one hundred thousand of the buggers by the time we land back in the UK next week.

That kind of word count is fine if you're recounting the adventures of the Dwarf King Spaffhammer and the Elf Queen Fairyhammock, as they trek across the great Minkel Pinkel Plains towards a final climactic confrontation with the Darklord Notasauronripoff.

It's also just about right if you're telling the exciting story of how Max Thunder - covert ops soldier and owner of colossal penis - stops the dastardly Russian plot to blow up the Midwest of America.

It's *not* the kind of length you want for a collection of musings from a neurotic English man, who's already half way through his first vodka and coke.

Anyway, I'd probably get to about seventy thousand words, run out of things to say and just start insulting all the people who have offended me over the years. This would be very therapeutic for me, but would probably lead to you demanding a refund.

So how's yourself, then?

Doing well since our last little tête-à-tête, I hope?

It looks like you've lost weight… well done!

The story about the gym in the first book didn't put you off exercise then?

That's good. Just because Spalding had a bad experience, it doesn't necessarily mean you will too. Though I wouldn't bet on it.

I haven't been exercising, but work has been pretty much non-stop, so I've lost a few pounds myself through stress – mainly due to looking at the clock on my office wall too much.

Work has been going quite well for me recently, though.

I haven't made any hideous mistakes and am 'winning friends and influencing people with my can-do attitude'.

17

I haven't shouted any anybody in weeks... unless you include the minor fracas I had with a junior designer in Reprographics last Friday. He thought it would be an excellent idea to change the subtle light blue I'd requested for a brochure with a garish *neon* blue that made the cover look like something from Tron. I remained relatively calm throughout our 'constructive' discussion however, and didn't resort to inserting a stapler into him even once.

Other than that, things have been peachy for me. Spalding's stock has been rising nicely.

I am being 'an important link in the chain'. My contributions are valued...

All this has resulted in the boss earmarking me for the honour of flying out to Australia in Business Class.

Also, I can't be a hundred percent sure, but I reckon he might've read Life... With No Breaks at some point, come to the conclusion I might write another book like it and thought it best to stay on my good side so I don't launch into a five thousand word rant about what a twat he is.

Don't worry Alastair, you won't be a target of my vitriol this time round.

Though what happens in a speculative third book all comes down to whether I get that pay raise next year or not...

Oh, *the power*!!

...just kidding.

I know how bloody lucky I am to be going to Australia for free - even if I will spend most of my time indoors, wishing the air-con worked better.

I also know how lucky I am that you bought my last foray into creative writing - so don't worry, I'm not about to start stomping round on a massive ego trip, pointing and laughing at the little people as I stride through the world like a colossus.

Mind you, I'm not going to lie and say I haven't felt a *slight* frisson of pleasure every time somebody has said a variation of the following to me in the past few months:

'Yeah... really enjoyed your book, Nick. Thought it was funny. Never knew you'd shit yourself in public. Er... if you write another one, you won't put me in it, will you?'

To which I'd generally reply with something along the lines of:

'Well, I don't know. It depends,' ...and leave it hanging there, offering them a sly smile and a waggle of the eyebrows for good measure.

The look of abject terror is priceless.

Not that being part of my ramblings is necessarily a bad thing.

Adam – my ex-wife Sophie's brother, if you recall - now has a wonderful anecdote to delight his friends with when he's down the pub. Talking about being in a book is far more interesting than banging on about the two foot trout you caught last time you went fishing in the Lake District.

Especially when the fish was more like *one* foot long and it happened *six years ago.*

Let it go man, for the love of God!

Sorry.

I've wanted to get that off my chest for ages now and it just came blurting out.

I was forced to go on that fishing trip and still haven't forgiven all those involved for making me do it. It's a tale of hardship and woe I still have trouble thinking about.

Okay, that's the first story sorted then:

It was six years ago and I was still married to Sophie. The ugly divorce monster was miles away bothering some other poor bastards and I was quite happy with my lot in life.

Adam called me one drizzly afternoon and asked if I wanted to come along on a fishing trip with him and his dad Malcolm.

Unfortunately I couldn't think of an excuse not to go.

I really, *really* couldn't.

I remember standing there for at least ten seconds with the phone to my ear, trying to manufacture some plausible reason why I couldn't go along, but my traitorous brain came up with nothing. I loathe fishing with a passion and can't think of anything worse than spending a weekend dressed in waders, cursing the invention of the weighted lure.

Having said that, my marriage was still fresh enough for me to want to make a good impression with Sophie's dad and as there was no decent excuse forthcoming, I agreed to the trip and hung up on Adam with a grimace.

I suppose if nothing else, the trip away might give me a chance to bond with Malcolm a bit...

Sophie's father is a massive tree trunk of a man, having run his own construction company for twenty five years. Most of his life has been spent labouring and sweating in all weathers, shifting huge piles of masonry and metal about, for what I assume were good reasons.

His arms are thicker than my legs. He can crack walnuts with his eyebrows. Midgets shelter under him in bad weather.

In short, he's built like a brick shit house.

I'm none of these things and am a writer by profession, so I'm therefore convinced he thinks I'm a homosexual.

Maybe two days spent depopulating the waters of Lake Windermere will bring us closer together and prove to him I'm not about to start singing show tunes and watching episodes of Glee on a loop.

The weekend of the trip duly arrives and Malcolm greets me with a doubtful expression as I walk up the drive to his palatial house, which nestles in a not quite rural area just outside town.

It's the type of neighbourhood where SUVs breed incessantly with one another and if you're unlucky enough to have credit card bills or an overdraft, you had better *keep bloody walking* until you're at least fifty yards beyond the last house in the village. Poor people are strictly not allowed around here, as they bring the whole vibe of the place down.

Not that those who live in this rarefied community are necessarily *posh*, you understand…

No, this type of village is full of otherwise ordinary working class types who just happen to have made good.

They know what it's like to be poor - driving around in a shitty second hand car, arse hanging out of a pair of seven year old jeans - and do *not* want to be reminded of it every time somebody roars past in an M reg Ford Mondeo. Poor people are a constant reminder of the bad old days and are to be avoided at all costs.

Paradoxically, despite the upturn in fortune, the nouveau riche can also find it very hard to let go of their previous down-trodden lifestyles.

These people can afford to visit the Maldives on holiday, but still go back to Benidorm twice a year because the food is good and the beer is cheap.

Eating in the most expensive restaurant for forty miles is easily affordable, but why bother when the Harvester round the corner is doing the Early Bird special?

If you're raised working class with no money, it can be bloody hard to shift up a gear, no matter how much cash comes your way.

Malcolm is a classic example of this.

He's become filthy rich from his successful construction company and mixes with the well-to-do all the time, but he still can't be bothered to get the anchor tattoo he's got on his neck removed. He just wears his Armani polo neck with the collar turned up.

He might have a Bentley Continental sitting on the drive, but it's filthy dirty, has fluffy dice hanging from the rear view mirror and there's a West Ham bumper sticker slapped onto it.

In a strange way I find it all quite admirable…

My fingers are just about left usable after he's crushed them in the vice that passes for his right hand.

'Morning Nick,' he rumbles.

'Morning Malc,' I reply, forgetting he hates to be called that and wishing I'd stayed at home in bed.

Malcolm lowers his walnut cracking eyebrows and crosses one meaty arm over the other, looking down the long drive as a car turns in.

Adam bowls up in his M reg Ford Mondeo, which has a blowing exhaust and no trim down the left hand side. He gets out of the wreck, revealing the fact he's wearing a very silly fishing hat on his head and an even sillier grin on his face.

'Morning! Ready to land some whoppers! Wahaay!' he exclaims, making what appears to be an obscene gesture as he does.

This is a disconcerting change in Adam's personality. He's usually a down-to-earth, sensible kind of bloke. That's why I get on with him. For some reason, the prospect of a day's fishing with his domineering father and reluctant brother-in-law has turned him into a lager lout.

'Morning son!' Malcolm booms.

Malcolm's default volume when he speaks is a boom. If you ever want the entire neighbourhood to know your worst secret, tell Malcolm what it is and ask him to whisper it to somebody else.

'Alright Adam,' I say in a tired voice.

Adam walks over and inexplicably puts an arm round my neck, catching me in a macho headlock I can't wait to get out of.

'Should be good, Spaldo!' He's never called me Spaldo before. 'Catch some fish, drink some beer, have a laugh!'

You can tell he's over compensating in the presence of his alpha male father. I'm fully expecting him to spit and grab his genitals any minute.

This speaks volumes about my chances of impressing Malcolm and getting on his good side. If his son feels the need to pretend he's a big, tough guy around his own dad, what chance have I got?

Adam has brought along some fishing gear for me as I have none of my own.

...I never will either.

Nor will I ever own golf clubs or a squash racket.

If you ever meet anyone who has all three of these things, run away as fast as you can. They're *bound* to be wankers of the highest order.

Malcolm ventures off to find his incredibly expensive fishing gear – no doubt stored carefully next to the golf clubs and squash racket – giving me time to grill Adam about the day's activities.

It turns out Malc doesn't want to just sit in a boat, dangle a line over the side and down some warm lager. Oh no, the progenitor of my wife intends to take us 'river fishing', which involved standing hip deep in freezing cold water, trying to catch one of the slower, fatter trout as it glides past on its way to mate with another fat trout somewhere downstream.

This will involve wearing waders.

Big. Fucking. Waders.

Adam produces my set from the boot of his car.

Because I'm the only one going on this trip who's sane enough not to be a hardcore fishing fanatic - and therefore owns no fishing equipment of his own - I get the hand-me-downs.

You know what wearing hand-me-downs is like, I'm sure. They always tend to be old, tatty and awful to both look at and wear.

The waders I'm being asked to don on this damp, cold Saturday morning are yellow. Not just a normal, run-of-the-mill, average, every day kind of yellow either. Oh no. These are bright yellow.

Seriously… *bright yellow.*

The kind of colour it physically hurts to look at.

I'm going to stick out like a sore thumb wearing these buggers. The local wildlife will have to put on sunglasses the second I step into their habitat.

Planes overhead will be able to use me as a navigation beacon.

There will be no chance of me catching a fish - even if I wanted to - as these bloody things will alert them to my presence while they're still swimming downstream in the next county.

A squidgy mass of thick rubber, they look like result of some carnal gymnastics between a pair of dungarees and the Michelin Man.

Due to their size, colour and the chill they still send down my spine whenever I think about them, they shall be henceforth known in this story as the 'Bright Fucking Yellow Waders'.

Capitalised for added effect.

…you're lucky I'm not writing it in bold too.

'Sorry mate, these are some of dad's old ones. He gave me them when I was a kid. They were a bit too big as I recall,' Adam apologies, trying very hard not to laugh.

'Really? And how long did he spend in prison for child abuse exactly?' I reply, taking the hideous Bright Fucking Yellow Waders with reluctance. This nearly gives me a hernia as it turns out they're incredibly heavy as well.

Malcolm comes back carrying his gleaming fishing rods. He takes one look at me holding the BFYWs and barks a laugh. 'Oh, you'll look lovely in those Nick!' he booms bombastically.

I'm now starting to think this entire thing is a set-up...

We load up Malcolm's brand new SUV with the fishing gear and begin the long and arduous journey northwards.

It's going to take several hours to get to Cumbria and I've already devised coping tactics to deal with the interminable trip. These include 'pretending to snooze', 'playing games on my phone' and 'reading the John Grisham I've been ignoring for months'. Unfortunately, Adam wants to chat the entire way and Malcolm decides to play his favourite jazz improv CD *very loudly*, so I have to almost shout to hold the conversation with Adam I didn't want in the first place. I have to wait for a lull in the hideous cacophony before I can properly let Adam know how his sister and nephew are getting on.

Jazz is shit. Especially that improvised rubbish.

It is. Just accept it.

It was invented by musicians who have no timing - and the buggers have been riding their luck for decades now.

By the time we roll into the Lake District park we're going to spend the weekend in, my brain has been reduced to the consistency of watery porridge.

I've also started to entertain a dark fantasy of dropping dead of a massive aneurism just to avoid having to put those terrible waders on.

The hotel Malcolm has booked is one of those that desperately wants to look like it's rustic and has been there for years, when in actual fact it was thrown up by an Eastern European construction company six months ago.

As we walk in to the foyer I notice on the display board that the hotel is currently playing host to a team building weekend for a well known telecommunications company. This cheers me up no end. Wearing bright yellow waders and listening to discordant jazz may be god awful, but at least I don't have to share a bedroom with Colin from Accounts, or take part in any trust exercises with the Reprographics department.

I have my own room in fact. This delights me no end and I can safely say this is the only thing that kept me sane in the course of the next couple of days.

I barely get time to settle in - no chance to fiddle with the trouser press while I make a cup of weak tea and eat the tasteless biscuit - before Malcolm is virtually bashing down my door, ready and eager to sally forth into the exciting world of fishing... which is an oxymoron if ever I heard one.

We get back into the SUV and drive *another* half an hour to what appears to be the coldest place on Earth.

The thermometer on the car dashboard says four degrees. It must be broken though as I'm sure it's actually minus sixty.

Malcolm and Adam jump into their waders with aplomb, gathering up their rods and tackle with happy looks on their ruddy cheeked faces.

I smoke three fags in a row, shooting an occasional glare of hatred at Malcolm's broad back and the yellow waders I know I'm going to have to put on in the very near future.

'Come on then Nick!' Malcolm's excitement about killing some innocent river dwellers has caused his already thunderous voice to increase in volume to near ear-splitting proportions. 'The fish are waiting for us! Get your shit together!'

I'm pretty sure the fish aren't waiting for us. I'm pretty sure the fish would like to avoid any contact with us whatsoever. I don't vocalise this thought because, as previously stated, Malcolm outweighs me by several stone.

…it's Bright Fucking Yellow Waders time.

Up to this point, I've been well aware of both the colour and texture of the monstrous garments. What I hadn't realised was the *size*.

I pull them on and look down in despair. It's like a small boy has got into his dad's wardrobe and decided to play dress up. The fact I'm also wearing the North Face body warmer my Nan bought me for Christmas a couple of years ago that's a size too big doesn't help matters.

I cinch the straps over my shoulder as much as I can, but the crotch remains at least six inches below my dangly bits and the waist sits just below my freezing nipples.

When I try to move, the billowing mass of rubber surrounding my legs rubs together, makes a squeaking noise like a mouse being molested with an egg whisk.

Walking like a sumo wrestler with rickets, I stumble to the rear of the SUV and gather up the worn fishing rod and tackle box Adam has also provided for this mini-break in Hell.

It takes Malcolm and Adam about two minutes to reach the river bank.

I get there in ten.

'Right Nick, shall I show you how to cast off?' Adam says. Malcolm's already striding out into the river, fighting the current. The look of expectant glee on his slab-like face is sickening.

'Yeah, alright,' I sigh, squeaking forlornly as I waddle over to him.

Adam shows me how to set up the fishing line, which I manage with little effort. He then demonstrates the correct way to hold the rod and line while casting off. With a deft flick of the wrist, he sends the metal weight and colourful lure out into the water a good twenty feet.

It looks easy.

I reckon I can get it to go *thirty* feet.

Copying his action, I flick the fishing rod back, gearing up for a really big cast that'll put his to shame. Unfortunately the line catches on a prickly bush behind us. I try to fling the rod forward as hard as possible, but it gets stuck half swing, causing me to lose my balance. Normally I'm a pretty well co-ordinated kind of guy and in circumstances where I'm not wearing Bright Fucking Yellow Waders ten sizes too big for me, I would be fine.

However on this occasion I *am* wearing Bright Fucking Yellow Waders ten sizes too big for me and therefore topple over, plummeting earthwards with a comic pin-wheeling of the arms.

I land heavily on my back, only avoiding serious injury because the thick wet mud breaks my fall.

However, because the waders are far too big for me, they've sucked up a healthy pocket of air during my slow waddle down to the river. As I hit the deck the air pocket is expelled in a loud, abrupt fart that echoes across the river like an anal thunderclap.

...yep, I'm the only person in the world who can start out on a fishing trip and end up being the world's first human whoopee cushion before I've so much as seen a sodding fish.

Adam manages to stop laughing long enough to help me back to my feet. 'I've never seen that happen to anyone outside a sit-com Nick,' he remarks with a chuckle.

Great, my life is now a re-run of a Terry & June episode.

To calm my nerves I smoke a cigarette and then have another go at casting. This time I curb my disastrous competitive instinct and after ten minutes I'm actually getting the hang of it.

'Right, I think you've got it,' Adam confirms hopefully. 'Join us out in the river when you feel ready.'

'Okay.'

It took another cigarette - accompanied by a long hard examination of my life up to this point - before I venture forth into the current, by which time Adam and Malcolm are both standing with intent looks on their faces, concentrating on the nylon lines plunged into the murky depths of the river.

This is a saving grace as it means I can stand well behind them and flounder around with my fishing rod, safe in the knowledge I'm not being watched. Additionally, Malcolm now has his extremely expensive waterproof Walkman on the go and is blissing out to the sound of his awful jazz.

In fact, Sophie's dad is having a whale of a time - no pun intended. He's landed three fat looking fish already.

Adam's only caught the one and I can see the tension setting in across his shoulders as the competition with his father heats up. I've caught nothing so far of course, other than a mild head cold and the attention of a passing orbital satellite.

Then, disaster strikes. I go and catch a bloody fish.

I'd been quite happily standing with the fishing rod tucked under my arm, calmly smoking and enjoying the weak sunlight filtering in through the low cloud. I'd even got used the current enough to lean slightly back, the enormous waders acting as a kind of stabiliser keeping me in place. I was, for the first time in many hours, at relative peace with the world.

This is not the correct state of affairs as far as the universe is concerned though and steps are taken to rectify the imbalance.

A trout, apparently depressed by the futility of its own existence, decides to get itself caught on my hook. This is made even more annoying by the fact I'd deliberately left the hook devoid of bait to stop this kind of thing from happening. I don't know what the stupid fish was thinking. Perhaps the dazzling glow of my yellow waders had bamboozled it so much that it stumbled into the hook blinded and confused.

Either way, I'm now stuck with the enormous slippery bastard.

I grab the fishing rod before the trout can snatch it from my hands and start to wrestle with it.

Adam notices what's going on. 'Fuck me! Spaldo's got a big one dad!'

He was thankfully referring to the fish, rather than the girth of my manhood. It would be four years before Adam would read all about my big wang in the pages of Life… With No Breaks.

Malcolm doesn't hear any of this as he's still got the Walkman on.

At this point, I should have just made some half hearted attempt to catch the creature to satisfy my audience. I had nothing against it and don't even like the taste of fish much, so in normal circumstances I would have been quite happy to pantomime a fight with the scaly monster before letting it go about its business. However, Malcolm and his son had left me feeling pretty emasculated with their robust knowledge of fishing, so my ego decides to wake up at this point, in an effort to redress the balance somewhat.

I figured that if I successfully landed my slippery new friend, I would sky rocket in Malcolm's estimations and he might object less to the concept of me inserting my penis into his lovely daughter on a regular basis.

I reel the fish in, really putting my back into it. Despite the trout's desperate attempts to get away, I quickly get him within reach of my grasp.

This is *brilliant*! I look like a fucking expert! The fish is a mere couple of feet in front of me!

I've caught the bugger!

...

...er, what do I do now?

I can't pull him over to the river bank on the line - he'll snap it long before I get there. Besides, progress in the massive waders in painfully slow and difficult when walking against the current, so the chances of losing my footing – and Mr Fish – are extremely high.

I now make the biggest mistake of the day so far... if you don't include coming on the trip in the first place.

I reach out my right arm, trying to catch hold of the enormous trout. He's literally a couple of feet below the surface of the water and within grasping distance - all I have to do is *bend down a bit.*

Now let's examine that last idea in all its glorious idiocy, shall we?

I'm standing in a good *four* feet of freezing cold Cumbrian river, wearing an oversized, heavy pair of waders that come up to my chest – which is about *five* feet above the surface of the water.

Bending down will lower me over *one* foot...

Done the math?

I fucking hadn't.

I reach down to secure the trout... allowing the river water to pour swiftly into the waders.

All thoughts of looking masculine and heroic are forgotten as the icy water envelopes my midriff and starts the highly unpleasant business of filling the waders from the ankles up. The bright yellow monstrosities may be old and worn, but they're still pretty bloody waterproof as it happens and the river that pours into them has nowhere to escape from.

I scream like a six year old girl and drop Adam's fishing line. He's a good twenty feet away so can't come to my assistance as the river empties itself into the waders, taking me off my feet.

Malcolm remains completely oblivious to all this, as he's still rocking out to the soothing sound of a group of musicians with no timing.

The air still trapped around my legs fights with the encroaching tide and I bob to the surface, flailing around like a harpooned whale.

The current happily takes me in its cold bosom and I float rapidly down river screaming head off – headed right towards where Malcolm is standing. He's facing downstream and doesn't know I'm coming.

'*DAD!*' Adam screams.

'MALC – *blubble* – OLM!' I shout, swallowing half the river.

Neither of us can get his attention.

...very bad things are about to happen.

I collide with Sophie's father, my legs neatly catching him around the waist in a scissor take-down Hulk Hogan would be delighted to execute.

Malcolm lets out a booming '*oof!*' noise that terrifies half the local wildlife in the vicinity and goes underwater.

I float over him just as he's trying to resurface and his head collides with my wader covered arse, applying more pressure to the water/air combination inside. I wader-fart loudly and let out another girlish scream.

Malcolm again tries to surface, this time successfully as I've now floated past him.

'What the fucking hell are you doing?!' he screams, causing a couple of nearby squirrels to drop dead of a heart attack.

'I was trying – *blubble* - to catch a big – *blubble* - fish!' I reply, trying not to drown as the equilibrium inside the waders finally goes in the water's favour and I start to sink.

Malcolm lets out several more expletives and grabs me around the neck, yanking my stricken body over to the far river bank.

Spluttering and coughing, I pull myself up the muddy bank. The waders are still full of water though, so I'm a good four stone heavier than usual and only manage to prevent myself slipping back into the water by clinging to a nearby tree stump for dear life.

The water pressure around my legs has built to such an extent that the waders now start to slide off, unravelling and stretching out into the water, threatening to pull me back into the icy depths. My screams would now make a six year old girl blush.

Adam has reached the bank and grabs one of the wader's straps cinched up over my shoulder. Malcolm grabs the other, still swearing his big fat head off.

The waders, having been subjected to a degree of stress they are ill-equipped to deal with, choose this moment to give up the fight. Both straps break with audible squelchy twangs.

Malcolm and Adam fly backwards into the mud, while the enormous waders get fully caught in the fast moving current and slip off my freezing cold body, pulling my sodden jeans down around my knees as they do.

The waders bob off down the river never to be seen again - much like my fishing rod and Malcolm's waterproof Walkman, which had fallen off during my water-borne assault on their owner.

Father and son slip and slide back to their feet and look down at me with matched expressions of utter disbelief.

Laying on the bank looking back up at them, the apologies start forming an orderly queue at the front of my brain.

I'm covered in mud, frozen to my bones, my Batman boxer shorts are exposed to the world and my body warmer is as ripped to pieces as my self-esteem.

As the weak sunlight blessed this holy scene from above, I resolved there and then that this would be the first and *last* fishing trip I'd be undertaking in my natural life span.

The drive back to the hotel was conducted in stony silence.

I remained in my warm, cosy room for the rest of the day, watching daytime television and counting down the hours until we left the next morning. I phoned Sophie to tell her all about what had happened, but had to end the call when she started having trouble catching her breath from laughing too much.

As I wallowed in misery all that afternoon - trying to resist the urge to order porn on the pay-per-view – Adam caught the one foot trout he's been trying to convince people was twice the size ever since.

Malcolm landed enough to open his own fish shop at the side of the road.

When they both returned that evening neither joined me for dinner, so I was mercifully spared the great tales of their fishing derring-do.

…or indeed *herring*-do, if you're in that kind of mood.

I went to bed that night secure in the knowledge that no matter what I did from now on, Malcolm was *never* going to like me and was never going to approve of me inserting my penis into his lovely daughter.

I'm sure if he ever entertained nightmares of me doing it from that day on, they would no doubt feature me molesting her in the Bright Fucking Yellow Waders - farting and squeaking my way to orgasm as I rolled around on top of her.

The drive home the following morning was conducted in bouldery silence.

That's like stony silence, only a great deal worse.

What capped the awkwardness of the journey was that Malcolm could no longer listen to his jazz, as the disc was now somewhere at the bottom of a river in the Lake District, keeping company with a pair of BFYWs and a fishing rod.

Malcolm has said precisely *ninety three* words to me since that incident.

I know this because I counted.

I can only imagine the rapturous joy he felt went Sophie told him we were getting a divorce.

The cry of delight he let out probably paralysed every small animal in a ten square mile radius.

**Somewhere over Kazakhstan. A place I have absolutely zero
knowledge of.**

What is it with me and having to start these books with hideously embarrassing anecdotes?

It's not false modesty, I assure you.

I guess it's just that embarrassing equals funny ninety nine percent of the time.

I could have started the book with the story of how I rescued a small dog from a drain, but there's not really much comedy mileage in a terrified puppy, is there? Even if you stick it in a tutu and a party hat.

Acts of kindness can elicit a positive reaction, but getting belly laughs out of them isn't on the cards.

It's best I stick to what I'm good at: detailing my humiliation for the purposes of getting a chuckle. It might not be all that dignified, but *'go with what you know'* as my English professor used to say, when he wasn't berating me for being a hack.

I suppose telling stories like that is also my way of ingratiating myself on you, if I'm honest.

After all, who wants to read a book all about how great somebody is? *Especially* if they're not famous?

You'd get about ten pages in and thrown the thing away in disgust – and quite rightly so. Ego-trips do not make a good basis for a book.

Pity nobody's told half the celebrities in our country that...

Hmmm.

Can you hear that fat bloke snoring a few rows away?

I knew he'd be trouble when we got on the plane. He looks the type who expects everyone to fall at his feet whenever he walks past.

I'm going to guess he's the CEO of a pharmaceutical company - though that may just be based on personal experience. Whatever he does for a living, I'm sure he's paid far too much and treats his staff like insects. The way he looked down his nose at the poor stewardess earlier was horrible.

Let's hope he chokes on a peanut during the flight - or suffers a massive coronary on the green at the thirteenth hole in a couple of days.

I find golf about as appealing as fishing.

The only reason I can't amuse you with an anecdote about it is because I've never played the game... and never will.

I like having lots of material with which to fill an observational comedy book, but you have to draw the line somewhere.

You can look forward to me recounting a story about inserting my John Thomas into an irate badger before you'll get one about me playing golf, such is my loathing of the sport.

I'm well aware that this opinion is probably in the minority, judging from the amount of golf related conversations I hear wafting through our offices on any given Friday afternoon. It seems that once a man reaches a certain age, salary and social standing, the desire to hit small white balls across a field becomes too much to resist. I'm sure there's something linked to sexual performance in that, but I don't quite know what it is.

I'll never get the chance to investigate, as I will never set foot onto the first tee for as long as I have small white balls of my own.

I suppose everyone needs a hobby, though. Otherwise the drudge of work – and the ticking of that infernal clock - gets too much to bear.

The dictionary defines the word 'hobby' as:
An activity or interest pursued for pleasure or relaxation and not as a main occupation.

Blimey, I never knew sleeping and wanking were my hobbies.

I wonder if there are any clubs I can join?

Living in an alienated society like ours – where we spend far too many hours working and far too few playing – means finding a decent hobby has become very difficult.

When you get to work at 8am and walk back in the front door at 7pm there's certainly no time left to dedicate yourself to more than one hobby, so picking the right one is vital.

There are so many activities out there to choose from, it's easy to get a bit confused.

I have chosen completely the *wrong* hobby recently - namely video games.

Here's a list for you:

Heroin
Cocaine
Nicotine
Alcohol
Angel Dust

Not one of these things is more addictive than Call Of Duty.

If you're unfamiliar with this particular video game (available on Xbox, PS3 and PC at the cost of your social life and personal hygiene), it's a shooting game in which you play a soldier from a first person perspective.

You're thrown into a series of confined arenas with 7 to 15 other maniacs from across our vast planet via the magic of the internet - and spend the next ten minutes doing your level best to shoot them in the face. You can play on your own or as part of a team, trying to win objectives and score more points.

Doing well at the game 'ranks' you up, earning access to more weapons and special attachments that make the game easier.

Doesn't sound so bad, does it?

…trust me, it's like crack.

I never played this kind of game before, but I've been a video games fan for decades.

You're looking at a man who owned both a Super Nintendo Entertainment System *and* a Sega Mega Drive, don't you know.

Through the years I've always been about the solo, story driven gaming experience, offered by such well known titles as Tomb Raider, Resident Evil and Uncharted.

Then one day last year I visited my friend Matt, who persuaded me to play Call Of Duty: Modern Warfare 2… and that was it, I was hooked.

I left his lounge at about three in the morning hyped up on caffeine and digital death.

The very next day I was in my local branch of Game picking up a copy, and went as far as cancelling a trip to the pub that night so I could stay in and play it.

Yes, I am a thirty eight year old man with a son and one marriage behind me, so I'm entirely aware of how sad this all sounds.

I can see you rolling your eyes and tutting.

It's not something I'm proud of I assure you.

I spend my working days dressed in a smart suit, holding important meetings with professional men and women; dealing with marketing contracts, business proposals and other exciting stuff… only to come home and spend three hours swearing like a football hooligan while a twelve year old boy from Nebraska shoots me in the head *for the eighth time in a row*.

I know I shouldn't be doing it.

Everyone else playing is at least fifteen years younger and twenty times more dextrous than I am, yet I can't help myself.

I even bought a headset the other day so I can shout obscenities at fellow players down my broadband connection while haphazardly spraying bullets in every direction.

In any other circumstance, telling a fourteen year old you're going to rip his fat little head off and shit down his neck would have you arrested in three seconds flat.

In Call Of Duty though it's not only tolerated, it's actively encouraged – especially if you're insulting what are colloquially known as 'noobs'. These are people new to the game, who run around like frolicking baby deer, getting riddled with bullets to the accompaniment of half a dozen lunatics screaming *'learn the fucking map!'*

I fear for the safety of any paedophile that attempts to groom teenagers while playing Call Of Duty.

They're all born cynics on there, spitting bile and vitriol at everyone not on their team. Any sex pest jumping on to chat up a kid while playing Domination would get their ears chewed off the second they failed to capture the objective because they were too busy asking 'x_x_RaZoR_BaLLs_x_x' what colour pyjamas he was wearing.

I guess I play the game because it's a good way to let off some steam at the end of the day.

I can't very well start taking pot shots with an AK47 at Mike from Personnel or Candice from Reprographics, so drilling 'Captain_Fartpants' with expertly timed sniper fire from behind cover is the next best thing.

Sadly, the time I'm able to dedicate to Call Of Duty is becoming limited these days, as I have a girlfriend and the chances of retaining her services will diminish greatly if I come across as a saddo who spends his free time playing computer games against teenage boys in another country.

What's that?

Did I just hear you say *'Quite right too'*?

Yes indeed, video games and girlfriends do not a happy combination make…

Uh-oh…

I can see the smile forming on your face and the look of anticipation in your eyes… you want to know how I met her don't you? I dropped that teaser at the beginning of the book and you've been waiting for the story ever since. The fishing trip anecdote was fine and all, but nothing beats a tale of romance - especially when Spalding's involved and there's likely to be a healthy dose of embarrassment to go with it.

As ever, you're the boss and I want to keep you reading, so here's the story in all its untarnished glory!

If you've read Life... With No Breaks you'll no doubt remember the sad tale of my marriage break-up.

It's been four years since it happened and you'll be pleased to know Sophie and I still maintain a cordial relationship with one another. She brings Tom round when it's my turn to look after him and we always have a good time chatting over our cups of coffee while he buggers around on his Nintendo DS (not playing Call Of Duty, I hasten to add), or runs around the garden chasing invisible monsters.

Sophie's floristry business hit hard times in the recent recession, but it's now starting to get back on its feet, which I'm as pleased about as her.

She complained to me the other day about the grey hair she's starting to find more frequently these days, but I still think she doesn't look a day over thirty.

Her tits continue to be fantastic.

And yes... she has read LWNB, in case you were wondering.

Surprisingly, my testicles remain attached to my body.

She wasn't *one hundred* percent impressed with the details of our courtship, marriage and divorce being read by thousands of strangers, but on the whole she took the contents of the book with good grace. The BMW buying story certainly made her chuckle, anyway.

Her first reaction to the book when I quizzed her was:

'Your cock's not that fucking big, Spalding.'

...which proves that while she looks like an angel, she can also swear like an alcoholic tramp.

Anyway, after our break-up, the idea of dating anyone else was a horrible proposition. Trying to wade in the murky, piranha filled waters of the dating scene filled me with about as much enthusiasm as contracting cholera.

I sank into a mire of singularity that lasted a good three years before a close female friend pointed out that dying alone is something to be avoided if at all possible.

It was time to get back on the horse... and go for a ride, as it were.

Looking round at my pizza box and porn filled front room, I conceded that she was probably right.

For a couple of months I sat back and waited for Miss Right to walk into my life.

Sadly, only Miss Wrong, Miss Married, Miss Neurotic, Miss Could Do With Losing A Few Pounds, Miss Ex-Wife and Miss Cleaning Lady Who Broke My Batman Mug And I Still Haven't Forgiven Her, crossed my path. There were simply no eligible young ladies in my vicinity.

———

…not surprising really.

There I was, a man in his late thirties with a broken marriage and slight paunch, working more than forty hours a week and socialising with the same group of inebriates, degenerates and lunatics I had for over fifteen years. With a lifestyle like that, the chances of meeting a new woman in the normal course of events were slim to none.

So Spalding started to consider something that would have previously been met with a raised eyebrow and derisory snort of laughter:

Internet dating.

Good heavens!

Internet dating is the domain of the terminally ugly and socially maladjusted isn't it? Not the kind of thing a thrusting young(ish) marketing executive in the prime of life needs to bother with, surely?

Even if he has got a slight paunch and rabid addiction to Call Of Duty…

This was my opinion of online dating when it was first suggested to me.

…a highly out of date opinion it transpires.

In the FaceSpace, MyBebo, TwitBook world we live in, internet dating has become a great deal more acceptable.

In fact, many would even argue it's a *better* way of meeting a member of the opposite sex than spending Saturday night in a club, getting deafened by terrible dance music, spending far too much money on watered down lager, and completely failing to pull even the shitfaced lass at the end of the bar, who looks like she'd suck off a tramp for another vodka and Red Bull.

Online dating is much more civilised.

You get a good impression of a potential mate before having to even be in the same postcode - provided they haven't lied on their profile like an MP when the expenses bill comes in of course.

Back in the day - before we had twenty four hour access to midget sex, movie ringtones and Perez Hilton – if you wanted to find love and didn't have the confidence to sally forth into the uncertain environment of the local discothèque, you had to put an advert in the 'Personal Ads' section of your local newspaper - hoping you wouldn't be the one unlucky enough to attract a mouth breathing rapist with halitosis and Tourettes Syndrome.

And woe betide you should it ever come to light that you were doing this, as admitting to looking for love via the printed medium would inevitably destroy your social life and make people think you were mental and smelt funny.

A quick aside… they still exist, the Personals.

If you have a bored few minutes, investigate the back pages of your local rag. There's a good chance you'll stumble across them somewhere.

I wouldn't actually go so far as to answer any of them though. The chances of finding somebody who *isn't* a mouth breathing rapist are probably very slim these days.

In the nascent years of the interwebs, online dating was treated in much the same fashion – the losers had just worked out how to use a dial-up connection.

Dating sites were almost exclusively populated by eighteen stone Brendas, nine stone Trevors, and the odd occasional Barry - who started off sounding quite nice, but inevitably turned out to be a mouth breathing rapist once you got past the opening pleasantries.

In our more enlightened and modern age however, millions of ordinary, well-adjusted people sign up all the time to the plethora of dating sites that abound.

We're pretty much all living disjointed three hundred mile an hour lifestyles these days, with no time for finding a decent new pair of jeans let alone a new lover, so is it any wonder that online dating has boomed in the way it has?

After all, you can find a used car, a new vacuum cleaner and a signed photo of Chris Waddle on the internet if you look hard enough, so why not love?

It took several weeks of constant nagging from his female friend to convince Nick Spalding of this fact though.

I still had visions of eighteen stone sexually frustrated elephants and mouth breathing sex pests running around my head… which would make the worse porno ever, come to think of it.

A constructive couple of hours spent on Dating Central one Sunday evening showed me the error of my ways however.

…and before we go any further, you should know that 'Dating Central' is a made up name, created to represent one of the more successful online dating agencies. My knowledge of slander and libel law is good enough to know that doing this a very *wise move*.

'Bloody hell, she's fit!' I would exclaim as I clicked through the list of potentials the search engine had listed for me using my carefully chosen parameters:

Women. Aged 25 – 35. Within 20 Miles Of My Location. Under 11 Stone. Full Set Of Teeth. Full Head Of Hair. No Psychopathic Tendencies. Nice Tits.

Of course, I never contact any of them…

That would mean spending thirty quid to sign up for the service.

Actually, you had to sign up for *six bloody months*, so it was more like ninety quid when you got down to it.

While some of the young ladies were attractive, none of them looked enough like Megan Fox to justify such a huge outlay of cash, so I shrugged my shoulders, clicked away from the site and surfed Porn Tube for an hour until I found a girl that looked enough like Megan Fox to wank over.

A couple of weeks pass...

Dating Central decides my email inbox isn't *quite* full of enough spam and starts to bombard me with updates, most of which feature new women in my local area.

Apparently my local area is the whole of Western Europe.

These mammoth listings are accompanied by the inevitable sales pitch trying to convince me that all I have to do to end my miserable existence of Tesco Meals For One and Sunday night wanking is to fork out nearly a hundred quid to buy into their service. As I work in marketing, this falls on very deaf - and extremely cynical - ears.

We're now into February and the single person's hell of Valentine's Day is homing into view like a rabid ninja in an eighteen wheeler.

This will be the third Valentine's Day spent on my own though, so the pain and self-loathing has been dulled somewhat by repetition. I plan on inviting a few mates round to watch something violent and misogynistic on the TV. After they've left I'll have a wank of course, as this is obligatory for a singleton on February 14th.

Then, miracle of miracles, Dating Central come up trumps and changes the course of Spalding's life forever...

I get yet another spam email, this one advertising a special Valentine's Day deal: A whole month's subscription for only £10.

Brilliant!

I can spend an entire month looking for the new love of my life, in the safe and secure knowledge it'll cost me less than a bad haircut.

I swiftly sign up and begin the long, laborious process of creating a proper profile.

I'd initially just bunged up some generic information without thinking about it when I signed up for the freebie account, but now I had to design an advertisement for myself that would hopefully make women come running like in that Lynx advert.

Hmmm... *problem.*

As stated above I work in marketing and for the most part I find it quite an easy job. I can wax lyrical about the delights of anything you care to put in front of me. Be it cat food, laxatives or a sports car, I'm your man for upbeat, inspirational bullshit that'll sell your product no matter how cheap it looks.

However, my unspeakable skills completely break down when trying to market myself. Neuroses, modesty and lack of self-esteem always get in the way.

I could write a more effective, attractive profile for Fred West than I could for myself.

Nevertheless, I struggle on with it.

The statistics section isn't too bad. That's just a series of drop down menus. It's a little hard to cock up your age, height, weight and religious preference.

I lie a bit of course. Everyone does.

I say I'm an inch taller and four pounds lighter than I really am. I've also miraculously turned into a man who enjoys regular exercise and cooking.

Then we come to the horror of the 'About Me' section. It says I have a maximum of 4000 characters to encapsulate how much of a dream date I am.

'Hi girls, I'm a writer with a big willy' is only 31, so I've got some work to do.

It takes me *three* days.

Three fucking days to write what amounts to two paragraphs of insecure fumbling I could have knocked out in ten minutes if it had been about somebody else - or a tin of dog meat.

It's a masterpiece of blandness.

In my effort to not come across as an arrogant prick - but at the same time attempting to sound like a confident go-getter - I write a load of neutral garbage only a woman from Switzerland would find attractive.

It's hackneyed, clichéd and reads like the profile of somebody trying to hide the fact they're a mouth breathing rapist…

Nevertheless, it's complete and I'm sick and tired of the whole thing, so I upload it before nerves get the better of me.

Now all I've got to worry about is the bloody photographs…

Deciding what to write in your description is bad. Trying to find a photo that doesn't make you look like an utter twat is ten times worse.

I'm not the biggest fan of having my photo taken because I never take a good picture, so the categories I have to chose from boil down to:

1) With Sophie on holiday. Obviously a non-starter. I don't want to do that thing where people post badly cropped photos that have their ex-partner hacked out of the shot, other than a cheek and half an eyeball.

2) When I'm shit-faced. Again, a definite no-no. I'm unlikely to attract a decent young lady if I slap up pictures of me smiling moronically at the camera in a dirty nightclub, tweaking a male friend's nipple with one hand, a bottle of Stella held aloft in the other.

3) Baby photos. There may be some cretins in this world who think it's cute to use these on a dating profile. I'm not one of them.

4) My passport photo. Yep, because nothing says 'eligible bachelor' like a seven year old photo of me staring straight ahead with a look of calculated murder in my eyes and several errant strands of hair sticking up at the back of my head, making me look like the world's crappest punk rocker.

My only - and I do mean only - other choices were a shot of me at a wedding in a passable suit and one taken at Christmas. I'm wearing a hideous jumper and holding a pen with a radio in it, but other than that it's not too bad.

Up they go on the site and I sit back and wait for the offers to come rolling in...

Funnily enough, this doesn't happen.

I do get one message from a forty four year old woman in Cleethorpes, who decides to tell me all about her day with her cat Mr Pancake, but as I'm not completely insane I delete it without responding.

Despondency sets in.

I call my female friend over (who incidentally doesn't want to be named in this book, so I'm now going to make one up for her... let's call her Babs from now on) and she sits down with me to see if a woman's perspective on my profile will help.

'You sound dull as hell, you muppet,' Babs says, swigging from the glass of Chardonnay I'd just poured her. 'You'll have to liven it up a bit. And that photo makes you look constipated.'

Babs proceeds to tell me what to write in the 'About Me' section and suggests a couple of pictures she has in her albums on Facebook.

Her suggestions improve the profile no end, it has to be said.

Gone are the comments about how I like to go for nice meals and enjoy long walks in the country. In are some actual references to my lifestyle, including my writing and the fact I play the guitar a bit.

Babs also insists I write some stuff about Tom, so I paraphrase a few sentences from Life... With No Breaks for inclusion.

I dutifully upload the changes she's suggested and within a couple of days I've been contacted by three women - none of whom have a cat called Mr Pancake.

While I'm apparently incapable of writing a good dating profile on my own, I *am* able to hold a decent conversation - even if it is by email - and I manage to ingratiate myself on some likely candidates.

To cut a long story short, within two weeks of placing my profile on Dating Central, I have my first date!

Dating etiquette tells us that the first one should always be somewhere public with lots of people, preferably during the day and kept nice and short. This makes the whole thing easier for all concerned.

There's no chance of getting kidnapped, and either party can get away easily if needs be - citing a need to get back to work, buy some shopping or go home and shave Mr Pancake.

The girl who's agreed to meet up with me is called Carla and I put some thought into an appropriate location.

I figure the local Café Nero sounds about right and fulfils the above criteria.

At a prompt one in the afternoon I meet Carla just outside the coffee shop and we go in.

It doesn't become clear that she's a complete lunatic for a good forty minutes.

All is well upon first inspection.

She's an attractive size ten brunette who looks like her photos and can hold a conversation without having to pause every sentence to breath through her mouth. She's also quite funny and has a witty turn of phrase.

Unfortunately, things take a definite turn for the worse when Carla starts to describe her childhood years spent in Kenya.

Carla, it turns out, is more racist than Nick Griffin.

This maniac would even make Heinrich Himmler blush.

When I make the mistake of asking her what her opinions are on the current levels of social depravation and political unrest in the country of her birth, she launches into a tirade about how all the trouble has been caused by uppity black people getting too big for their boots.

I sit there in uncomfortable silence while she entertains me with the sad story of how her family were virtually forced out of the country.

Uncomfortable silence turns to horror as she describes how parties of machete wielding locals went around hacking up white people, including her next door neighbour.

I can see why all this would have an understandable effect on her, but the depth of her hatred towards the indigenous people is beyond the pale.

She only manages to get the word 'nigger' out twice before I decide I've got some very important paperwork to do back at the office.

———

41

If I had a cat called Mr Pancake, I'd sure as hell be getting off home to give him a good shaving right about now.

I leave Carla sitting with a rapidly cooling second café latte. I'm very pleased I hadn't ordered her a black coffee as she would probably have tried to lynch it.

The second date is with Francesca.

Francesca is French - but let's not hold it against her just yet.

For this date I decide on one of the more picturesque pubs in the area.

It's the kind of establishment that feels it necessary to nail old bicycles and ploughs to the ceiling for reasons which I've never entirely understood, but it's on my route home from work and is quite popular with the locals, thus ensuring Francesca's safety in case I'm Peter Sutcliffe in disguise.

Francesca also looks like she does in her photographs.

…from the neck up.

I come to understand why she'd only included head and shoulder shots in her profile when we meet. Francesca is much like an iceberg – there's a lot more going on down below.

But I'm a twenty first century man and being a size eight to ten isn't everything. Perhaps Francesca will be a delight to talk to, mitigating the extra couple of stone she's got clinging to her midriff.

She does laugh in the right place when I make a joke about the bicycle nailed to the ceiling, which is a good sign.

Then, as it's nearly eight in the evening, Francesca of course decides to order some soup.

I mean, why wouldn't you order soup on a first date with a complete stranger? What could possibly go wrong?

'Zo Nick,' she says, lips pursing round the spoon. ''ave you been on 'oliday anywhere nize zis year?' *slurp*. 'I went to Egypt lazt month.' *slurp*. 'Eet woz beautiful!' *sluuuuuuuuuurp*.

I can't think of a response, completely transfixed as I am by the slurping - along with the fact she's now huddled protectively over the bowl of green lentil soup like Gollum.

'I alzo luv ze south of France.' *slurp*. 'I go zere with my family every zummer,' *slurp*. 'You should go zere if you can,' *slurp, slurp, slurp*.

I just about managed to hold onto my dinner while she consumed the rest of the soup.

Francesca then asked to go outside for a cigarette.

I'd recently quit, but wasn't one of those rabid ex-smokers who despise the very sight of the little white tube, so I agreed to stand outside in the cold with her while she blackened her lungs a bit more.

Now, as stated, Francesca was French and therefore smoked French cigarettes. Gitanes, to be exact.

She sparked one up and this was where the date really went south for me. I'm well used to the smell of cigarette smoke, but the stench that rolled out of that fag was like somebody had set fire to a wet bison.

My lunch, which had successfully stayed down during the Lord Of The Rings soup extravaganza now really threatened to make a reappearance as the Gitanes fragrance assailed my poor nasal cavities.

She blew out another stream of fetid smoke and I leaned forward to get underneath the noxious gas as it billowed over my head. Francesca misinterpreted this completely and thought I was moving in for a cheeky kiss. She smiled and opened her mouth, gearing up for a smacker.

Her teeth were… *strange.*

They were set at random angles to one another, like a graveyard after an earthquake. They were also tinged ever so slightly green.

To avoid the horror of having to connect my mouth with one that smelled like burned bison and looked like a set from the latest Hammer horror movie, I feigned a coughing fit. I may have gone overboard with this as Francesca started to slap me on the back with urgency as I bent over double.

I stood straight again and caught the small look of disappointment on her face that indicated she knew damn well I'd faked the cough to avoid kissing her.

…dating can make you feel quite *awful* sometimes.

I didn't run out on Francesca that evening the way I had the card carrying member of the BNP, but I did look at my watch every five minutes for the rest of the date.

I was profoundly glad to say goodbye to my new French friend in the car park at about nine thirty - no kiss for obvious reasons - and drive away at some speed…

Third time lucky, right?

Hell no!

In her profile picture Sandy looks about twenty eight, nine stone and had a wealth of auburn hair.

In real life she was forty eight, seven stone and had a ginger fright wig you could have cleaned your pots and pans with. It was like someone had unravelled a Brillo pad and painted it orange.

I'm running out of inspiration when it comes to choosing dating locations by now, so I meet Sandy back at the bloody Café Nero.

It's a pity we didn't go to Starbucks because I believe they have an OAP discount rate.

I try my hardest to engage Sandy in conversation out of politeness, but when she starts going on about her grandchildren I know it's time to conjure up some more very important paperwork that absolutely *has* to be filed in the next ten minutes.

I have no idea why people engage in this kind of thing…

I'm all for posting a profile and picture that makes you look good, but please have it represent who you actually *are* for crying out loud.

There's no point in uploading old photos or fakes.

If you're planning on physically going on dates with any of the people you meet, you're going to get found out sooner or later - unless you tell them you have a pathological aversion to being seen in public and conduct the entire meeting with a bucket on your head.

This will probably guarantee you won't get a second date as much as lying on your profile.

Before leaving, I asked Sandy when the photo was taken. She at least had the decency to look a little shame-faced when she said *'Nineteen ninety two.'*

Not the most auspicious of starts to my online dating career, I'm sure you'll agree.

In fact, after three disasters in a row, I pretty much give up on the whole thing. I was now over three weeks into the month long deal anyway, so I figure I've had my shot at finding love via broadband – and have failed dismally.

It's been an altogether unpleasant experience and I shall never be able to look at a bowl of lentil soup or a Brillo pad the same way again.

I vow to chat more women up in future when I meet them in bars, to avoid this kind of thing happening again.

Then, some four days before the subscription expires, I get a brief email from a girl calling herself 'Willow81'.

It simply says: *'Hiya. I like your profile, it made me laugh. Let me know if you fancy a chat.'*

There's not a mention of how her day has gone, how many times she's had her heart broken in the past, how her friends all refer to her as being *bubbly*, or how she likes to take long walks by the sea.

All good so far.

Her picture is brilliant too.

Not because it makes her look like a model who's just stepped off a catwalk, but because it's been taken at a party, with her looking to one side, not even aware the camera is on her. She has one finger twirled in her hair and a half smile on her face.

She looks effortlessly beautiful.

I respond to the email, mentioning some of the things she talks about in her profile and trying to be as charming as I can within the confines of an electronic message.

I obviously don't make any horrendous *faux pa* as about an hour later she responds. We then spend the rest of the evening exchanging emails.

I remember that I'd had plans that night for a marathon catch-up session of House, my favourite TV show at the time. There were six episodes stacked up on the Sky Plus box - which gives you a good indication of how busy I was at the time - and I had every intention of watching them all that evening.

In the end, I didn't get round to seeing one.

This girl had completely captivated my attention - even if it was only over a broadband connection.

By midnight we have to sign off because of work the next morning, but the last thing we do is trade real names. Hers is Jenna.

She suggests that I download MSN Messenger so we can talk on that next time, as it's far quicker than the email system Dating Central employs.

It takes me a couple of days to work out MSN properly, but eventually we're chatting every night. My Dating Central subscription lapses and I don't even notice.

I'm starting to think this one is a real winner.

Happily for me, it looks like she thinks I'm not so bad either and we agree to meet up at the Starbucks in town (her suggestion) at 2pm the next day.

Jenna looks like her pictures, from the tips of her toes to the top of her extremely pretty head.

During the date she doesn't order soup, seems to like everybody - except politicians, local radio DJs and her landlord - and our conversation isn't broken once by one of those uncomfortable pregnant pauses that indicate a second date probably won't be on the cards.

She's quite tall – about my height – and has a lithe slim figure I find it very hard to stop staring at.

Much like my ex-wife, she has lovely tits.

Match this with legs that go on forever and an extremely cute mole above her lip - and Nick Spalding is in first date heaven.

We end up staying way longer than I'd planned and the pile of *genuine* paperwork I have waiting back at the office is completely forgotten.

I don't try to kiss Jenna goodbye at the end of the date. I don't want to push my luck. However, I do nervously ask her out again and she agrees - much to my fragile ego's relief.

The second date - a meal in a country pub which I spring for - is even more fun than the first, despite getting our cars locked in the pub's car park at the end of the night.

By the time the third date rolls round I'm starting to entertain the idea that I might be entering in to a new relationship for the first time in well over a decade...

That was over a year ago now and I'm pleased to say Jenna and I are still getting on like a house on fire.

We haven't argued once, spent three weeks together on holiday in Australia without getting on each other's nerves and recently celebrated our one year anniversary with a meal in the same pub we visited on our second date, followed by some extremely pleasant bedroom shenanigans that I'm sure as hell not telling you about here.

I'm *very* glad we've reached this point in the relationship as I'm never comfortable with those first few tentative months.

All that tedious pretending to be cooler than you really are gets quite stressful after a while. I understand why it's necessary, but I'd much rather just proceed straight to the one year mark, when your partner knows you're not cool in the slightest and has heard you fart at least once.

Anyway, I had no chance of coming across as cool, did I? Not when I've written in detail all about how I shit myself in public.

It's a little hard to be a stud around your new girlfriend when she has ready access to a book chronicling just about every embarrassing episode of your life.

No matter what I say or do Jenna just has to fire up her Kindle, load her copy of Life... With No Breaks and flick through its pages for a couple of minutes:

Spalding: 'Yeah Jenna, I run two miles every day. My body is a temple.'

Jenna: 'Bullshit. You've been on a treadmill once and it nearly gave you a heart attack.'

I'm trying my best to mitigate the colossal damage I've done to my image and relationship stability with flowers, chocolates and by improving my oral technique.

If none of that works, I might try going to the gym again.

Healthy people are attractive people I'm led to believe.

Jenna's now read all of Life... With No Breaks and enjoyed a majority of it. She even cried at the part where Sophie and I broke up.

...yep, she's definitely a keeper.

In fact, she's the real reason you're reading *this* book.

Jenna's the one that persuaded me to write a sequel and suggested a great time to do it would be while I was flying to Australia on business.

Therefore, please address any emails of complaint to her, instead of filling up my inbox - which several people did last time round when they took exception to my views on organised religion.

...ahem.

My helpful friend Babs met Jenna for the first time last month when I invited her round for a meal. Babs had been away working for nearly a year and was desperate with curiosity to meet the new woman in my life.

I'm pleased to say they got on very well.

This is vitally important to a relationship.

Friends and girlfriends have to like each other if you're going to have an easy life, I find.

After a bottle of Pinot Grigio Babs thought it would be absolutely *hilarious* to regale Jenna with tales of how pathetic I was at online dating, as well retelling a story from my childhood that makes the crapping myself in public one from LWNB look tame.

In summary retaliation I will now reveal that 'Babs' is really Amanda Bentley, 36, from Southampton. She lives in a rather nice semi-detached house in the village of Warsash with her husband David. Amanda once threw up into her own knickers while sat on the toilet in Martines nightclub in Portsmouth.

See Mandy?

I warned you telling that story would come back to haunt you.

Let this be a valuable lesson to you – and a healthy reminder to any of my other friends who might be thinking about doing something to embarrass me.

I have something you don't: *an audience.*

6.12am GMT
14665 Words
Over India. The happiest people I've ever met have been Indians.
They must know something I don't.

Very true.

I defy you to walk into an Indian restaurant anywhere and not be greeted with a warm, happy smile.

There's been a lot of talk in our country in recent years about the high levels of immigration, and while I can see the point that the influx of Europeans may not have helped matters in the past decade, I refuse *point blank* to accept that inviting the lovely people of India, Pakistan and neighbouring countries has been anything other than a massive benefit to the citizens of the UK.

They work indecently hard, always provide a quality service and are an honourable, friendly bunch.

Some of the spineless BNP supporting apes who spout hate and prejudice against them could do with adopting their work ethic and approach to life.

Sorry, a high horse moment there. I apologise.

Jenna is a big fan of curry, so I've been visiting a lot of Indian restaurants lately.

She's whip-thin and couldn't put on weight if she tried, but I'm older, slower and have a metabolism like shifting continental plates, so have to be careful not to eat too many keema naans and chicken jalfrezis.

Right now I think I'm about one curry away from a much needed diet.

I still haven't managed to shift the weight I put on after quitting cigarettes, so I might be back down the gym in the near future – whether it makes me look like a spandex wearing prick or not.

Yes, I have indeed managed to wean myself off the ciggies.

They are forever gone from Spalding's life, never to return - unless something really bad happens or they invent ones that don't kill you.

On a twenty four hour flight like this, I'm eternally glad to have overcome my addiction.

In previous years, I would have been climbing the walls by now, having been locked in this metal tube for over eight hours.

The need for nicotine would have been all consuming and this entire section of the book would have just consisted of *'all writing and no cigarettes make Nick a mad boy'* written over and over again, Jack Torrance style.

But that isn't the case. Spalding has finally kicked the demon weed.

Hooray!

It got to a point last winter where I had phlegm you could hang wallpaper with, a persistent cough, and the unlovely knowledge that I was getting closer and closer to forty - the age at which things like prostate and colon cancer can really begin to kick in.

The self preservation gene must have activated, because I started looking at every cigarette as an enemy and resolved to quit as soon as I was able to muster up the will power to do so.

As I promised in the first book, I didn't tell anyone I was giving the little nasty buggers up. Neither did I set a special date.

Instead, I hoped that a time would come in the very near future where I'd sneak up on my own subconscious and surprise it into not having another fag.

Thus it was on a cold January day last year, after I'd emerged from a meeting with a client in Winchester, I sparked up a Marlboro Light, coughed like a seventy year old asthmatic and looked in disgust at the £5.35 price on the front of the packet.

I decided there and then that enough really was enough for one lifetime.

…and I haven't smoked a cigarette since.

It wasn't all plain sailing of course. The six dismembered corpses under my patio will attest to the fact.

Just kidding.

It's only five.

I can't say I've noticed any of the *wonderful* effects that ex-smokers tell you all about when they quit.

I haven't sensed any change in my ability to smell things, food doesn't taste better and I still wheeze a bit if I have to climb more than two flights of stairs.

I do have a lot more change in my pocket these days though and don't have to leave the pub every half an hour to stand outside in the freezing cold with all the other future cancer patients.

I'm also completely insufferable around other smokers now.

I figure if somebody as lame and weak-willed as me can quit smoking, then it can't be that hard. Everyone should be able to do it.

Hence my complete intolerance when any smokers have the temerity to spark one up in my presence - and my utter distain when between lungfuls they moan that they can never kick the habit.

Poppycock and balderdash!

If I can do it, so can you, Smoky Joe!

The same goes for sexual positions…

I have in my repertoire precisely *five* sexual positions, plus a series of variations on each theme that aren't really different enough to be considered unique. They are as follows:

Missionary
Doggie style
Cowgirl
In a chair
69

I'm sure there are more, but I'm way too far along in life to learn any new ones now.

I flicked through the Karma Sutra once, but some of the pictures looked about as sexy as herpes.

Why they thought a series of drawings depicting a bloke with a big bushy moustache shagging a fat lass was a good idea is beyond me.

I'm also convinced they actually ran out of positions after the first five like me and just busked the rest.

Changing your grip from her thighs to her ankles does *not* constitute an entirely new position in my book. Neither does making her bend over the dining table rather than the kitchen counter.

Anyway, I figure if I'm capable of performing the five positions listed above, every man on the planet should be able to do them.

There are no excuses, lads!

The same goes for sporting prowess…

I am about as sporty as Stephen Hawking, but even I can bowl a cricket ball in roughly the direction of the stumps, kick a football in the general vicinity of the goal, throw a dart fairly close to the treble twenty if I'm sober, and jog a mile without my lungs jumping out of my chest.

These should be the bare minimum requirements for anyone who wants to be considered a step-up from being a fat, lazy bastard.

If you can't do these simple physical tasks, you're in trouble.

The same goes for pub quizzes…

Everybody loves a pub quiz, including me. Sadly I'm shit at them.

I'd like to think my general knowledge skills are up to snuff, but the chances of me answering more than ten questions in the average Wednesday night quiz are slim to none – even when one of answers is invariably 'the blue whale'.

If you can beat me in a pub quiz, consider yourself a step above completely hopeless in the general knowledge stakes.

I really do think I should be used as the yard stick by which others are judged - because believe me, the standard I set *isn't* high. Most people can clear it at a jog and anybody who can't should be lambasted and publicly humiliated.

They should make me the benchmark for humanity. The test by which the six billion on this planet can get a better idea of their place in the pecking order.

If you can't even pull yourself up to Nick Spalding's low standards, there's definitely no hope for you…

…

Oh dear.

I've depressed myself now.

There's nothing like being reminded of your considerable shortcomings to bring the mood down.

I don't think it helps that I'm pretty knackered.

Haven't slept a wink so far and the copious cups of British Airways coffee I've been drinking are no longer maintaining my concentration.

Therefore, in a marked difference from Life… With No Breaks, I'm now going to take a break and have a quick nap.

It's only a couple of hours until the first leg of our journey ends with a short pit-stop in Bangkok, so I'm going to save what I've written so far (checking I've done it properly at least four times before closing the document window), shut the laptop and try to snatch some shut-eye.

Feel free to join me… and just ignore it if I start talking in my sleep. It's something I've been doing recently.

My girlfriend informed me the other night that I had a short, but vitriolic conversation with Katie Price while fast asleep where I called her a 'plastic tit monster' - proving that even in a subconscious state, I can spout opinionated rubbish about people who annoy me.

I apologise in advance if I start slagging off Paris Hilton between snores.

So then, by the miracle of the narrative chapter device I will speak to you again in the time it takes for me to have a snooze and for you to flip to the next page.

8.03am GMT / 3.03pm Local
16167 Words
Bangkok airport. Not a lady boy in sight, which is something of a disappointment.

Ugh.

You know I said earlier I don't take good photos? My passport photo is ample example of this.

I look like a serial killer with a broom handle shoved up my arse.

I've just had the indignity of going through Thai border security (even though I'm not leaving the airport... how does that work?) and had to suffer an uncomfortable few seconds while the pretty Thai customs officer tried her level best not to laugh as she compared my haggard face with the thirty one year old version of it stuck to the back page of my passport.

There's always a quiver of dread that goes through me when an official is scrutinising my passport photo.

I never know whether it's best to just let my face relax, or try and approximate the same expression as the one I'm making in the mug shot.

I don't have a broom handy most of the time though, so I tend to settle for the first option in the hope that I still look enough like me seven years ago for them not to think I'm trying to sneak through on some other bugger's passport. I can do without being hauled off to a dark room for a strip search and some rubber glove romance, thanks very much.

Even though it's been seven years I still remember how much money I spent getting that passport photo done: £5.

Yes. I had *five* separate attempts to take a halfway decent photo, and the serial killer / broom handle look was unbelievably the best one. It was a toss-up between that and the shot that made me look like I'd just eaten a pound of Mogadon. The coin came down heads, so broom handle it was.

I know this all makes me sound like a massive narcissist, but I knew damn well at some point in the future a pretty Thai customs officer would be looking at the photo trying not to laugh and I didn't want to make the task any harder for her. The £5 was well spent in my book.

Right then...

We're now sat in the clean, sterile environment of the airport waiting lounge as the plane is refuelled and they restock the peanuts.

———

53

The chairs here are those ones that look quite comfortable from a distance but are in fact horrendously hard and unyielding when you get up close and sit on one.

The building itself is an enormous steel and glass tube, vaulted with criss-crossing metal pylons that create a vague spider web effect, and gigantic sheets of canvas that look like they could detach from their moorings at any point and drop onto my sweaty head.

The hot Thai afternoon can be viewed through a multitude of huge glass windows and judging by the heat haze shimmering off the runway and palm trees beyond, I'm very glad that somebody invented air-conditioning.

Behind me I can hear the dulcet tones of an electronic woman's voice warning people in no uncertain terms that the end of the travelator is 'lapidry apploaching'.

I know I shouldn't find her accent funny, but shame on me and curse my soul I still do.

Usually I find the Thai accent quite musical and pleasant - when it's coming from a real human being, that is. When it's piped via a tinny intercom system every time a passenger cuts an invisible laser beam however, I just can't take it seriously. The poor girl sounds like an Asian Dalek with anger management issues.

...yes, I wish the small oriental child sitting across the way would stop staring as well.

It's very disconcerting and is quite frankly ruining my concentration.

It's hard enough to write a coherent narrative when you've had no sleep and you're sweating like Pavarotti on a treadmill, without being studied like a bug under a microscope by a boy in a Pokémon t-shirt.

...oh good grief, he's picking his nose now.

I really don't need that. Neither do you, I'm sure.

I may have a son of my own, but this doesn't mean I take any great pleasure in being around small human beings of his ilk. They tend to be sticky, noisy and unavoidable.

I'm going to shuffle left in my seat to get out of his eye line...

...sadly this has brought me into view of a large blonde gentleman wearing *extremely* tight blue shorts and a yellow polo neck that his chest hair is trying its hardest to escape from.

He *must* be German.

The aviator sunglasses perched on his head aren't doing anything to improve his image, nor is the fact he's sitting with his legs as wide apart as is humanly possible. I can't quite tell whether he's circumcised or not, but could take a good guess.

The fact he's in Bangkok leads me to make some assumptions that may or may not be correct about his sexual proclivities.

Next to him are two fat British people.

I can tell they're British because he's wearing an England top from the mid nineties and she's got a pair of those stupid 'jeggings' on that are doing a nice job of highlighting just how flabby her thighs are. He's bald and she's got lank dyed red hair. Both have faces liked a slapped arse.

Only two British people could look that miserable in a fascinating, exotic country thousands of miles from the nearest speed camera and Tesco Express.

Oh no… the child's moved and is back in my eye line.

He knows he's freaking me out, I'm sure of it.

It's not the nose picking that's weird *per se*, it's the accompanying thousand yard stare that's giving me the creeping heebie jeebies.

I wish his mother and father would put those bloody iPad's down and move him away.

They're both sitting over there, occasionally prodding the screen like a dog in one of those behavioural experiments. It's pathetic really.

Give it a thousand years and humans will have evolved flat vertical pads on the ends of their fingers to make screen prodding easier on the nerve endings.

I'm going to stare back at him for a while to see if that puts him off.

…

Yep, that did it.

The little bastard's now climbed onto one of the concrete hard chairs and is bouncing up and down trying to draw his parent's attention away from Angry Birds.

Good luck with that pal, that bloody game's even worse than Call Of Duty.

Thank the lord…

They've just called the first class passengers, so the rest of us cattle will no doubt be re-boarding soon. Actually, I suppose I'm only semi-cattle being in Business Class.

This is officially a *good thing*, because my arse is really starting to ache. I bet yours is too.

I'm also impatient to get on with this flight.

I'm not in love with the heat trap that is Bangkok in mid afternoon enough to want to stay here much longer.

Still, you don't have to sit here and suffer with me for a moment longer, my friend. That e-reader you're holding is like a time travel device. Just pop along to the next chapter and the half an hour or so it will take for us to get airborne will pass in the blink of an eye.

I'll see you on the other side of the long queue now forming at the gate!

Over Vietnam. Not America's favourite place, I'm led to believe.

Damn it.

It appears the lovely stewardess we had on the first leg of the flight has been replaced by her mother.

…who appears to have eaten all her other children.

She's just asked me if I need anything and I had to resist the urge to say *'please bring me some snacks before your will power breaks.'*

I'm bloody glad the two British people from the waiting lounge are back in economy, otherwise the plane would be front heavy and we'll be ploughing into Ho Chi Min City like a gunship in 1964.

Americans may well be offended by that last remark, given that they understandably don't want to be reminded of that dark chapter in their country's past.

Still, at least they managed to learn their lessons from the Vietnam War and have never again invaded a sovereign nation for reasons which were morally murky at bes-

…aah.

That's awkward.

Let's just put it down to the fact George Bush was a lunatic and leave it at that, eh?

I still prefer him to Tony Blair. At least Bush had a set of balls on him.

Balls which led to an illegal war that's killed thousands of innocent people - but big hairy Texan balls nonetheless.

Blair is just a snivelling little dweeb who did anything the big boys told him to so they wouldn't beat him up.

Bush shouted:

'JUMP!'

…and Blair answered:

'How many brown people do you want me to kill?'

What a colossally embarrassing period in Western history that entire debacle was.

It ruined our reputation across the world and helped sink us into an economic recession we're not likely to get out of until the ice caps melt.

Thanks Tony!

It wasn't like we - and by we I mean us pasty British people - needed to get involved anyway.

America has enough military hardware to fight ten consecutive world wars and scarcely needed the contribution of the already ailing British military - but up jumps Tony with some blather about weapons of mass distraction and in we merrily trot, hanging on to the ankles of our American cousins as they blasted limbs and heavy metal across the Arabian desert.

It would have been so *easy* to let them get on with it on their own. Maybe then we wouldn't have the highest unemployment figures in history, a fucked public sector and a pathological aversion to anyone whose name ends in Ali.

Thanks Tony!

I never bought the whole 'War On Terror' thing either.

I know a bullshit bit of corporate branding when I see it.

We spent billions every day trying to topple Saddam Hussein - who had bugger all to do with 9/11 - while the beardy twat who was actually responsible sat in a cave somewhere in Afghanistan hardly able to believe his luck.

I am, by my own admission, something of an idiot when it comes to common sense, but even I know they should have been spending all that cash on finding Bin Laden.

I eventually had to stop watching the news throughout the early noughties because I'd find myself shouting at the television every time Sky gave us an update of how many soldiers had been blown up by IEDs in Baghdad that week.

I'm not saying Hussein was a nice bloke - of course I'm not, he had a small moustache after all and they're never a good sign - but it seemed a tad silly to plunge headlong into an extended conflict with him when the nutter we really wanted was squatting under a bush somewhere between Kabul and Islamabad.

It's kind of like finding out the local bully has beaten up your best mate and you retaliate by burning his next door neighbour's house down.

Of course Bin Laden wasn't squatting over a major oil field, which may well have had something to do with it...

Not only are we seen as warmongers who stick our noses in where they aren't wanted, we're also perceived as a bunch of greedy bastards with the morals of an alley cat.

Thanks Tony!

The Europeans had the right idea.

The Germans - who have a great deal of previous when it comes to this kind of thing - stayed well out of it. The French have never exactly been keen on armed conflict - even when the aforementioned nation was trundling through their vineyards in 1940 - and also kept quiet.

Same goes for the rest of our European cousins... and who can blame them? The whole enterprise looked like a wrong 'un from the outset.

They all sat back with their arms folded and watched the invasion happen live on Sky News, the lucky bastards.

I hate Sky News.

Sorry, but I do. The twenty four hour news cycle means there's a constant need for new stories and Sky aren't shy about dredging up any old topic they can think of, and sensationalising it to the point of absurdity:

Has your town got a bit of a problem with drug dealers?

Well, Sky will come in and make out there's a druggie scumbag on every corner, preying on pensioners and generally making the place look untidy.

Had a man arrested in your local area for owning two indecent images of children?

Sky will *assure* you he's just the tip of the iceberg and that there's a paedophile hiding in every bush waiting to take your first born.

Yes... I mean **THAT BUSH**. The one by the side of your house. There's a sex offender crouched there *right now*, holding a razor blade and a copy of Mein Kampf, waiting for you to turn your back for a millisecond so they can spirit your child away to their sex dungeon...

Had a few bus shelters vandalised in your street by kids?

Oh no, no, no... that's not nearly exciting enough.

Let Sky News take you on an odyssey of horrific (and possibly fabricated) stories about hoodie wearing evil teenagers who will rape your corpse just as soon as look at you!

Okay, I'm exaggerating for effect, but I hope you get my point.

...there is a paedophile in the bush by the side of your house though.

I'm blaming Sky News because they're one of the worst – and most high profile – offenders, but all those buggers are at it to one extent or another.

The world can be a bad enough place without the media blowing everything out of proportion just to fill the 2am to 3am slot, when every right thinking individual is fast asleep anyway.

The print press are as bad, if not worse.

They've had plummeting readership figures since twenty four hour TV news came in and will do just about anything to sell their papers to the audience that's left.

I love the way the local rags try to keep up with the big boys and find enough stories to fill their pages.

The tragic March 2011 earthquake and tsunami in Japan was a good case in point.

One local newspaper in my area actually ran the story: *'What would have happened if the tsunami had hit us!'*

Yep, they did an entire feature on what damage would have been caused to the south coast of England if the tsunami had hit here - instead of several thousand miles away on the other side of the world... in a country that's actually *on* an earthquake fault line.

Now, I don't know if anyone told them this, but the news is supposed to be about reporting *factual* information to the public about the various important matters of the day. It is *not* an excuse to print an entire page of complete bollocks on an event that is categorically *impossible* and would never, *ever* happen in a million, billion years.

Good grief.

They followed this legendary piece of journalism a couple of days later by interviewing the only Japanese person living in the area about his feelings on the disaster (he was delighted, as you can imagine) and then proceeded to speak to a boring couple who'd recently been on holiday in the country.

Yes, they interviewed two people whose knowledge and emotional attachment to Japan was entirely based on a week long vacation - most of which was probably conducted under water.

I'm all for trying to find the 'local angle' but that's going a bit far, isn't it?

I was tempted to send the paper an email asking them if they'd like to speak to me as I'd eaten my own body weight in sushi the night before and had a valuable contribution of my own to make.

Here's the problem though... and it's the same one that keeps companies making terrible products at Christmas time:

They wouldn't keep writing / broadcasting this crap if *we* didn't keep buying into it – and *believing* it.

The reason why papers like The Daily Mail keep trying to make us believe there's a sex offenders in every bush when there quite plainly isn't (though there is one in *your* bush... that's the absolute truth), that drug dealers stand on every corner infecting society with their filth, and that you'll die in hideous agony on a bed in some dilapidated NHS hospital corridor, is because *we* keep buying the fucking papers they print that rubbish in.

We've become a nation - and arguably a whole planet - of gullible pricks, implicitly trusting the word of journalists, even though they all have an agenda to sell papers or get higher viewing figures above all else... sometimes at the cost of the truth.

At some point in the past we stopped believing what the politicians were telling us - for the good of all humanity - and started questioning what they had to say.

I wonder how long it'll be until we do the same with the media?

I'm afraid it'll probably be around the time the ice caps melt, killing off all life on Earth...

...including the bush that paedophile is hiding in **RIGHT NOW. HIDE YOUR CHILDREN!**

I had a run in with a local reporter some years ago that will probably get my point across better than any of the above blustering diatribe.

It goes something like this:

Back when I was still one third of a nuclear family with Sophie and Tom, we lived happily in our three bed semi-detached house. The property not only benefited from GCH and being close to local amenities, it also featured a rather nice landscaped front garden.

A central feature of this attractive plot of land was a small collection of garden gnomes.

Two of them already existed in situ when we bought the house, but I ended up adding a further three in an orgy of carefree spending at the local garden centre.

You may not think I sound like a garden gnome kind of guy, but when I explain that they were garden gnome versions of Darth Vader, Hitler and the Stay Puft Marshmallow Man, you might understand their appeal to me - and why I couldn't get the credit card out fast enough.

The gnomes took pride of place next to their more conventional cousins, who sat on a mushroom and held a fishing rod respectively.

All five lived in splendid harmony for a whole year, before the crime of the century occurred.

One warm summer's eve, Darth, Hitler and mushroom gnome were stolen!

The evil monsters left fishing rod gnome and Stay Puft for some reason - maybe because they ran out of arms, or maybe because they didn't enjoy Ghostbusters and once went on a fishing trip to the Lake District they didn't want to be reminded of.

Regardless, the next day I step out of my front door to enjoy a Sunday morning cigarette and the crime is revealed to me.

I was incredulous.

Who the fuck steals a garden gnome?

I reported the crime to the local fuzz and began the long, slow process of mourning the little stone bastards.

It was hard.

Hard I tell you.

A week passed and I was just about getting over the trauma.

Part of the healing process was a lovely afternoon snooze on the new comfortable couch DFS had provided us with a mere day before.

My blissful rest was rudely disturbed by the sound of the door bell.

Bleary eyed and quite cross, I get up and answer the door to a skinny young man in thick black glasses, a dark blue cagoule and look of mindless enthusiasm.

'Good afternoon Mr Spalding!'

I'm immediately on my guard. Anytime a complete stranger knows my name it makes me suspicious. They're either about to issue some kind of summons or tell me a relative has died.

'That depends. Who are you?' I find it hard to keep the irritation out of my voice.

'My name's John Wilkie,' he says, proffering a hand for what turns out to be a disturbingly limp hand shake. 'I'm a reporter for the local paper.'

'Right...' I'm now reaching behind the front door, trying to put my hands on the stout wooden walking stick I keep there.

'Just wanted to speak to you about all these gnome thefts.'

That stops me in my tracks. 'You what?'

'All the gnome thefts?' he repeats, pulling out a note pad expectantly. 'I've been told you're a victim.'

A victim...

He's calling me a 'victim' because somebody pilfered three stone midgets from my front garden.

'Been a lot has there?' I ask, despite myself.

'Oh my yes! At least seven people in this area have lost gnomes over the past few weeks.'

He's been following this story *for a few weeks*. There's actually so little news going on that a reporter is forced to keep track of somebody nicking garden gnomes.

Unbelievable.

'So it's a big story then?' I ask.

His eyes light up. 'Well, they're thefts aren't they? People are coming onto your property and shamelessly stealing your gnomes. It could just be the tip of the iceberg!'

'The tip of the iceberg?'

'Yes! If they can do that... what else do you think they could be capable of?' His voice lowers to suggest that these heinous criminals could be capable of *anything*. After all, when you get right down to it, there's really not *that much* of a leap from stealing garden gnomes to committing rape is there?

Until now, this conversation has just left me confused. As John tries to suggest that gnome theft is the first step on a criminal career that will probably end with being hanged for treason, confusion turns - as is inevitable - to anger.

This jumped up little prick is committing the same sin as Sky News and all the other media outlets – exaggerating a problem just to make people scared in their beds and keep newspaper sales buoyant.

My hand closes over the walking stick... and then loosens again as I change tack.

I could beat this bottom feeder to death on my doorstep, but this would lead to a change in lifestyle I'm ill equipped to deal with. I've never had to bend over in a prison shower before and have no desire to change that fact.

Also, Sophie might not appreciate having to bring Tom up on her own.

Displaying a level of self control I would have otherwise thought impossible when rudely awakened from a soothing nap, I relax and decide I'm going to have a little fun with this dweeb.

I effect as pained and mournful an expression as I can muster.

'Oh! It's awful!' I exclaim, melodrama oozing from every pore. 'You're absolutely right Mr Winkle,'

'Wilkie.'

'Wilkie. To think those evil bastards invaded my privacy and brutally stole my garden gnomes out from under me!'

'Absolutely!'

'I mean, what's this country coming to, eh? When a man can't keep a lovely collection of tasteful garden gnomes in the front rockery for passers by to look at and admire?'

He's *loving* this. 'Can I quote you for our piece, Mr Spalding?'

'Of course you can! I'm glad my story can be told.' It's time to ratchet things up a bit. 'Those gnomes had great sentimental value to me.'

The pen scritches across his notepad at three hundred miles an hour. 'Did they? Why?'

This is where I decide to see how much bullshit I can feed this bloke before he realises I'm stringing him along.

'Well, the gnome on the mushroom wasn't very valuable, but Darth Vader and Hitler meant the world to me. They were a gift from my grandmother.'

His eyes light up even more. He's *knows* what's coming. 'Is, is your grandmother no longer with us, Mr Spalding?' he says, having a really good try at genuine sincerity.

'Yes, yes she's passed.' I bow my head. 'It was such a tragedy how we lost her.'

Scritch, scritch. 'And how was that?'

'She exploded.'

The pen stops. I'm trying my hardest to keep a straight face. Thankfully I manage it, otherwise the end of this anecdote would be rubbish.

'She… she *exploded*?' he said, looking understandably suspicious.

I effect an even more tragic expression. 'People never believe me when I tell them, Mr Milkie.'

'Wilkie,' he corrects automatically.

You can see what's going on in his head… he's trying to decide whether I'm a lunatic, or a genuine grieving grandson with a golden story to tell.

He plumps for the latter. 'What happened to her?'

'She was in Mexico. A big fan of guns, was my Nan. It stemmed from her time in the WRENs during the war I think. She ended up going to some illegal shooting range out in the desert, because they said she could have a go on a 50 calibre sniper rifle.' He's actually writing this down. 'There was an accident involving a box of hand grenades. One of the local bandits got drunk on tequila and starting mucking about. My Nan was standing too close they said…' I pause and work an emotional catch into my voice. 'There were bits of her everywhere!'

'Wow, Mr Spalding. That's a very sad tale.' He actually has the good grace to stop writing for a second. 'No wonder the gnomes meant so much to you. Was anyone arrested for her death?'

Un-*fucking*-believable. I stifle a laugh by pretending to choke back a sob.

'No… no, the authorities tried, but no-one was ever caught. I spent months down there with the Federales trying to track him down. They say he probably blew up as well. Bastard!'

Wilkie shakes his head. 'Very, very sad…'

There's a brief pause.

'Can we get a photo of you holding one of the remaining gnomes for our paper?'

What a prick.

Two days later I walk into my local newsagent and pick up the morning edition.

On page seven is a half page story about the gnome thefts. There are three pictures accompanying it.

One is a small black and white shot of John Wilkie looking smug, one is a map of my local area with stars marking the various gnome theft sites… and the third is a shot of me in my front garden, dressed in my faded green flannel dressing gown. I'd insisted on wearing this for the photo as it's the tattiest piece of clothing I own and makes me look like Arthur Dent's alcoholic brother.

I have a look of abject misery on my face and I'm clutching the Stay Puft gnome to my chest as if it were my first born.

It's the only photo ever taken of me I genuinely love.

I would have used it for the online dating profile, if Babs had let me.

And the story's headline?

HOW COULD THEY TAKE DEAD GRAN'S GNOME GIFT?

Brilliant.

Not only is it utter bullshit, it's alliterative, unpronounceable bullshit!

Wilkie even went as far as to report that my Nan had been 'sadly killed in an accident while holidaying in Mexico'. I was rather upset he didn't go with the exploding granny angle as…

GRAN GOES BOOM, LEAVES GARDEN GNOME

…is a much better headline, even if it doesn't quite rhyme.

I dined out on that particular piece of creative deceit for quite some time.

It's one of those rare occasions where Spalding got the upper hand, so I try to bring it up at every opportunity.

I have no idea whether anyone believed the story or not when it was published, but I'm deathly afraid that at least a few probably did.

There's a level of trust still handed out freely to members of the press that is unfortunately abused all the time in the drive to maintain profits.

My only advice to you is: believe nothing, question everything and don't take a story at face value just because Jeremy Thompson tells you it's true.

…unless he's warning you about that paedophile in your garden bush. Aaaagghh!!

11.46pm EST
20933 Words
Over East Timor (more or less). Is there a West Timor? Or North? Or South?

I can see the face you're making, you know.

You're thinking the sentiment of that chapter was little a hypocritical, aren't you?

I shouldn't really be having a go at journalists for bending the truth, when I'm pretty much doing the same thing in this book to make sure these stories are funny.

This is a valid observation, I won't argue. I do occasionally embellish a little bit to make a tale more chucklesome.

But:

This book is a piece of entertainment and not like the news - which is supposed to remain impartial, objective and *accurate*. You can't call it *news* otherwise. The purpose of it is rendered pointless.

…it's a pity the major media outlets of the world seem to have forgotten that.

Tell you what, I'll stop being a pontificating prat now and return you to your regularly scheduled entertainment, okay?

Speaking of which, let's have a look at what wonderful in-flight goodies are on offer during the rest of the flight, shall we?

Writing the book is taking up nearly all of my time obviously, but I need a break every now and again, and there might be something interesting I can distract myself with as the creative juices refill.

Give me a minute. These in-flight TV menus are a real bugger to negotiate sometimes. The fact the touch screen has a one second delay on it every time I prod the flaming thing doesn't help. Especially considering the fact my patience runs out in roughly half a second.

Right, here we go. I've found the movie menu.

Hmmm…

The selection isn't brilliant – as ever.

The King's Speech wasn't bad… but that Red movie with baldy Willis was all mouth and no trousers. Tron Legacy made my eyeballs ache and Black Swan suffered from a severe case of pretentious twaddle-itis. The less said about Gulliver's Travels and The Tourist the better.

Those are the new releases.

I'm not even going to bother with the selection of 'classics' they have on offer, because I'm one hundred percent sure half of them *won't be*.

Invariably in these circumstances I've seen pretty much every movie available anyway.

It's an affliction every true movie fan can sympathise with, and the reason why most of us don't bother subscribing to Sky Movies.

By the time a film gets 'premiered' we've already seen it twice and have spat out a critique on the nearest online film forum. There's not a lot of point in forking over £30 a month for a movie channel if you've already seen everything it's showing at the cinema or on DVD months ago.

Some people also chose to download pirate versions of the latest flicks from the myriad torrent sites freely accessible on the interwebs… depending on how loose their morals are.

Piracy is *not a good thing* of course - in the movie industry or any other entertainment form. We all know this.

People labour and sweat for years over their project, making every effort to create a fantastic piece of entertainment… only to have it pirated by unscrupulous gits across the web, denying them rightful pay for their talents and effort.

…well, more or less anyhow.

If the above statement were completely true then there would be *no* excuse for piracy and anyone who's ever done it could consider themselves guaranteed a one way ticket to Hell – where they would spend eternity with my great uncle Gerald Shearwater.

But let's examine the first part of that statement for accuracy, shall we?

People *labour* and *sweat* to make a *fantastic* piece of entertainment.

Really?

All the time?

For *everything* that comes out?

…because I don't know about you, but I've seen some truly epic shit at the cinema in the last few years that makes me strongly question the commitment of the film makers.

You can bleat on about how bad pirates are until you're blue in the face, but keep churning out movies like Transformers 2: Revenge Of The Horrific Racial Stereotypes and what do you expect?

I spent thousands of pounds on therapy to block out the horror that was Indiana Jones and the Kingdom of the Crystal Skull. I hate that film so much, I'm dedicating an entire paragraph to it, centred and in bold.

And that's the central point.

There's a massive amount of hypocrisy going on here.

On one hand the movie companies are pleading with us not to pirate their product, while on the other hand they're raising prices at the cinemas and churning out film after film of contrived, unoriginal rubbish to bash us over the head with.

What exactly do they expect?

Yes, piracy is bad and costs jobs. I'm not promoting its use and don't condone those who engage in it - but let's *try* to have a balanced view of the subject, please?

We're being constantly gouged by movie companies who couldn't give a flying fuck about making a quality product, or charging a fair price to see it.

At some point, people are bound to take steps...

I'm fully aware that doing away with piracy altogether isn't on the cards, but its effect could at least be mitigated by providing films worth getting off your arse and paying to see.

It's *ten pounds* to watch a film in the UK these days - and that's just for the ticket. Add the cost of parking, snack food and transport and you can't watch the latest blockbuster for anything less than *twenty* quid all told.

Prices are also on the rapid increase in the USA as well.

Is it any wonder more and more otherwise law abiding folk are happy to let their morals slip a bit to watch a pirate copy of Toy Story 3 at home - for *free*?

To whit, here is Spalding's message to Hollywood:

Dear Hollywood,

Want piracy stopped? Want us to fork out our hard earned wages on a trip to the local multiplex? Want us to support your multi-million dollar industry?

Then stop making terrible movies that are targeted solely at hormonally challenged American teenage boys.

Stop executives interfering with the director and the writer's vision just because you're terrified of doing anything new. Take a fucking chance once in a while... you may be pleasantly surprised.

Also, lower your prices to a level that will encourage attendance. I'm no fiscal expert, but I'm sure halving the price of a movie ticket now and again will get more bums on seats and mean less profit is lost to the pirates.

Stop the concessions charging a small fortune for sweets and popcorn, as well. Get them down to average street prices and that'll encourage even more people back to the cinema. Especially the fat ones.

And for the love of God, somebody take Michael Bay out into the backyard and shoot him, please.

Yours, Nick Spalding.

P.S: The film rights to 'Life…With No Breaks' are now available.

Ok, that might be going a *bit* far (we could just kneecap Bay and leave it at that) but the point stands, I reckon.

What the hell has happened to the movie industry?

I know there have always been bad movies, but it seems that in recent years the ratio of bad to good has sky rocketed to ridiculous proportions in favour of the negative.

Me and a mate of mine thought we'd catch a flick the other day and I went on the internet to check out the reviews of recent releases.

Of the seven or so movies we'd actually want to watch only *one* had more than a 50% rating on Rotten Tomatoes.

That's not great – and a subsequent bit of research uncovered the fact that the ratio didn't get much better across the whole year. The past *decade* was even worse.

Have a look yourself the next time you have a spare moment. The drop off in quality over the last thirty years will make you wince.

I can count on the fingers of one hand the amount of films I've genuinely enjoyed at the cinema in the past decade - and three of them were directed by Christopher Nolan.

If all those reviews had been written by the above mentioned American teenage boys then I'm sure things would be different. That really is the only audience Hollywood seems to cares about.

The rest of us are left swinging in the wind, trying to convince ourselves that Avatar was a good movie.

Which of course it *wasn't*.

For many and varied reasons… not least of which was the fact it caused me to upchuck my vastly overpriced hot dog and bucket of Sprite.

Oh goodie! Here comes a story about vomit:

Being the most hyped and promoted movie in history, Avatar was virtually required viewing by everybody with a heartbeat, whether you wanted to see the thing or not.

So I find myself one cold December evening before Christmas in a queue outside the cinema longer than a Bangkok prison sentence, with my mother, sister, brother-in-law, niece, nephew, sister's next door neighbour, her husband, their son, his girlfriend and Osama Bin Laden.

The last one is a lie, but the bugger might as well have been there, it seemed like everyone else in the world was.

Eventually, after an entire hour spent standing outside Nando's looking at their menu (turns out they cook a lot of chicken) we shuffle forward into the cinema proper to buy our tickets and vastly overpriced hot dogs and buckets of Sprite.

Added to this is the excitement of the 3D glasses.

A spotty herbert doles them out to everyone and before long most of the queue either look like Stevie Wonder or a reject from The Matrix.

The acne ridden cinema staff then throw the doors open to the biggest screen in the house, letting the cattle in.

I make a beeline for the best seats – the ones in the middle at the front of the main block. I only have to knock over one disabled seven year old girl to do this, which for me is a good result.

I hate getting bad seats - be it for the cinema or on a plane - and will do my utmost to secure the best in the house before anyone else. Woe betide you if you're between me and Row A, seat 12… especially if the movie is over three hours long.

I get comfortable - as do my family and friends, who have followed in my swathe of destruction and managed to grab the rest of the row.

I'm already halfway through my hot dog by the time the preview trailers kick in and I've also put a good dent in the bucket of Sprite.

Now, the last time I remember going to the cinema to watch a film in 3D was to see the legendary masterpiece that was Jaws 3.

We're talking the early eighties here, so it's been a long time since I've experienced the gimmick. I don't remember suffering any problems watching an unconvincing rubber shark eat even more unconvincing actors all those years ago, so have no reason to believe that watching Avatar in the same manner will be in any way problematic.

How wrong I was…

The film begins and frankly, it's shit.

I don't claim to be any kind of movie critic, but even I can spot a thinly-veiled rehash of Dances With Wolves featuring giant blue smurfs and acting just this side of a heavy oak cabinet.

I turn to my sister to point this out but she shushes me in a very abrupt manner. The story appears to have completely captured her imagination. Past her, my mother looks bored to tears, once again reinforcing my opinion that I am more like her than my siblings.

I remove the stupid 3D glasses for a moment and take a quick look around the cinema.

It's like the Blind Association is in town. And all of them are popcorn addicts.

There's one lad in the far corner with his glasses off and a grumpy look on his face playing around on his iPhone. I don't usually feel much camaraderie with the youngsters of today, but right now I'm totally with him.

Nevertheless, I've re-mortgaged my house to watch this bullshit, so I rejoin the crowd, turning my attention back to the movie with shades in place.

It takes another ten minutes for unpleasant messages to start coming from my stomach.

It's a particularly exciting part of the film, where one of the giant blue smurfs - who's really a human - has jumped on a big pink dragon thing and is swooping around an enormous oak tree with an expression of stupid delight on his face.

If you're lucky enough not to have seen Avatar yet, this does indeed look as stupid as it sounds.

As the camera ducks and weaves with the blue smurf's progress around the technicolour background, I start to feel *very* peculiar.

For the next quarter of an hour I sit trying to convince myself that I *don't* feel sick and have *no* need to rush from the cinema to the nearest toilet.

Sigourney Weaver's grandmother is blathering on about something to do with caring for indigenous races and how the evil humans need to be stopped before they strip mine the giant blue smurf people's land, but I'm paying virtually no attention as the only thing I'm interested in stopping is the gorge rising from my stomach and re-introducing my hot dog and Sprite to the outside world.

I lose the battle as the little bloke from Saving Private Ryan starts shouting at the meat head from Clash Of The Titans.

…we've all done the vomit run.

It's never conducted with dignity.

All pretence of social etiquette disappears the second you feel the unpleasant warm rush of liquid and diced carrots flooding up from the back of your throat, demanding egress from your body.

Thank god there were no seats in front me, otherwise the 3D spectacle of James Cameron's latest effort would have been somewhat ruined for the person in front by my hot sick running down the back of their neck.

Instead, I was up like a shot unimpeded, striding past my rapt family with my left hand clasped firmly over my gob trying to stem the tide…

I could feel the bile starting to seep between my fingers as the up-chuck really tries to get into full flow.

As I run down the corridor and bang the doors open, my stomach gives another lurch and sick spurts simultaneously upwards and downwards, going up my nose and down my jumper.

It's like when you put your finger over the end of a hose.

Now, I'll pause here… to ask if you're feeling sick yet?

I apologise if so, but if I'm going to recount an anecdote about throwing up in public, I might as well be up front about the details. Besides, I have to top a story about shitting myself in public here, so I'm cheerfully falling back on the gross-out tactics to do so.

Mercifully, the men's loo is only one screen along and I reach it before the chunder can completely win the battle.

I stumble through both toilet doors and rush towards the nearest sink.

Reaching it, I let the full force of the nausea take me, spraying a hot, constant stream of vomit into the sink that Mr Creosote would have been proud of.

'YYAARRCCHHUURRGGGHHHHH.'

That's the *exact* noise I made.

I wasn't happy.

…nor was the ten year old boy who'd been washing his hands in the sink next to me.

The poor bleeder had just popped in for a post movie wee after watching Where The Wild Things Are and just happened to be in the wrong place at the wrong time.

Not that I hit him directly with it, you understand. He just caught some of the backwash.

Which is still enough to ruin your day, I have to admit.

He let out a screech of revulsion and I was suddenly very aware of being a thirty six year old man in a public toilet with a small screaming boy.

'I'm so sorry!' I cry, wiping spittle from my lips. 'Did I get you?'

'Mum!! Dad!!' he wailed, waving two vomit speckled hands out in front of his body.

With hands outstretched, limp at the ends with terror, the boy ran towards the toilet door looking and sounding like one of those velociraptors from Jurassic Park.

Once he'd disappeared I turned back to the sick filled sink and turned the tap on, trying to get rid of the evidence. Thankfully it wasn't too 'chunky' and a majority of it went down the plug hole.

I washed my hands and walked out of the toilet in desperate search of a mint.

Outside, sickboy was standing with a man and a woman who must have been his parents. He had his little face turned up to theirs in anguish, hardly able to articulate what had just happened to him. This was just as well as dad looked quite big and more than able to wipe the floor with Nick Spalding should he decide to do so.

Both parental units had their backs turned to me, so I crept back towards the screen trying my hardest to look inconspicuous.

I went back through the double doors with relief, only to bump into my mother who'd been coming the other way.

She was evidently the only member of my poxy family that had decided my welfare was more important than the giant blue smurfs.

'Are you okay Nickle Pickle?'

'Please don't call me that mum.'

'Aren't you feeling well?' The concern in her voice is partially touching, partially embarrassing. I'm in my mid-thirties, let's not forget.

'Just er... feeling a bit sick, mum.'

'Was it the hot dog? Those things are awful, you know.'

Now she's thrown a seed of doubt into my head.

Until now I'd been convinced that the 3D was responsible for the nausea, but maybe it was the hot dog.

There was only one way to find out...

I followed mum back into the screen just as the big CGI tree owned by the giant blue smurfs was getting blown up by that actress who always plays a Hispanic lesbian soldier.

I sat back in my seat and retrieved the glasses from the floor in front of me.

Putting them on I turned my attention back to the movie, just as several big shiny flying battleships start strafing the tree, sending the camera swooping and shaking and-

...nope, it's definitely the fucking 3D.

I'm up again and the 100 metre vomit sprint is back on!

Thankfully sickboy and his parents have left the vicinity as I come banging through the double doors again, so I speed toilet-wards without fear of violence against my person.

I make it to the actual toilet stall this time, spending a constructive five minutes getting completely rid of the hot dog and Sprite, as well as the chicken and bacon baguette I'd had for lunch, the three bourbon biscuits I'd had for elevenses, the bowl of honey nut cornflakes I'd had for breakfast and the bag of jelly babies I ate when I was seven years old.

At least that's what it felt like, anyway.

Throwing up like this is perfectly fine when you've been out all night on a bender. You've contributed to your own downfall, so can't really complain too much when your kidneys are trying to exit through your mouth.

You *don't* expect this kind of treatment from your involuntary bodily functions when all you've done is make the mistake of paying to see a movie about giant blue CGI smurfs in loin cloths.

To this day, I have no idea what happens at the end of Avatar.

Even in my nauseous state I could tell that the whole thing was bloody silly and I've never felt the urge to pop a blu-ray version into the PS3 to see what all the fuss was about.

I've also never ventured back into the cinema to see one of the thousands of 3D movies that have spawned since Avatar made five trillion dollars at the box office.

Yes indeed, in lieu of decent movies, Hollywood has fallen back on making everything shiny and three dimensional to get your arse on a cinema seat - and not pirating everything in sight at home to save yourself some cash.

Well done guys!

What's the next tactic? Just have someone just stand in front of the screen with a set of keys, jangling them up and down for the morons to look at?

'Look everyone! Look how shiny shiny they are! You don't need a plot that makes sense, decent characterisation or attention to detail! Shiny shiny!'

Come to think of it, I don't know what makes me feel sick more – the 3D, or the contempt that Hollywood has for anyone with half a brain cell.

Sorry, that turned into a bit of an anti-Hollywood rant.

It just really pisses me off when my intelligence is insulted - especially when it's being insulted by people exhibiting a less than adequate level of intelligence themselves.

I know I'm probably shouting at a brick wall, but it's nice to get these things off your chest.

Which - as ever - is the real point of this book.

I can't afford weekly therapy sessions on my wages - and this is by far and away the next best thing.

I thoroughly recommend it if you're stressed about anything. Just sit down and spill it all out on the page.

Who knows? Maybe you can publish it and rake in a few quid like I have.

I seem to have a never ending list of things that annoy me to a greater or lesser extent. I must have been born with the tolerance gene missing from my DNA.

Take this for instance:

A couple of weeks ago, somebody vandalised my lovely BMW.

…yes, the same one.

I had to park it down the street a bit as some utter bastard had taken the space outside my house - I had words later, don't fret.

So at a chill 7am, I walked down the street to the car and saw with horror that the nearside wing mirror had been kicked off.

Admittedly not the crime of the century, but very annoying nonetheless - and also pretty expensive, once you take into account how much labour I get charged to fit a replacement part. I'm stupid enough to still be taking the car to the proper BMW garage in the city, guaranteeing prices far above what I'd be charged at a local mechanics.

Anyway, the wing mirror has been kicked off and I'm *bloody livid.*

I live in a nice residential area, where the drug addicts have the decency to do it behind closed doors and the only time a prostitute turns up is when she's been brought here from the docks by a punter.

There are no paedophiles hiding in any of our bushes.

Nevertheless, some teenage git or drunk idiot has bashed the wing mirror off at some point overnight, leaving it hanging forlornly by a single wire. There's also scratch damage to the door, compounding the disaster.

In a fit of pique, I do something that's very much out of character and will probably do me absolutely no good in the long run.

I call the police.

This is - of course - a total waste of time.

The government of this great nation has seen fit to stretch the police force (and I do mean *force*... it's not bloody *service*) so thin, the term *transparency* can be used in more than one sense of the word when describing the local constabulary's relationship with the public.

The chances of a copper turning up if it's *you* that's been booted in the face - rather than your wing mirror - are slim, so the odds of me getting a response to this heinous act of criminal damage are infinitesimal.

However, I am extremely angry about the whole thing and need to vent. Somebody with a collar number and bad hand writing is going to get a piece of my mind today.

The call handler at the other end of the line goes through the motions as I describe the scene to her. I've been watching way too many cop shows recently and have always taken an interest in police procedure, so she gets very fed up with me saying stuff like: 'I can't see any scuff marks from shoes on the car or pavement, but you may want to send CSI down here to check it out. Stat.'

I can't even keep my emergency services terminology straight in my rage.

She cuts me off just as I'm starting to explain the visibility conditions and likelihood of epithelials being left by the suspects.

'Thank you for the information, Mr Spalding. We'll pass your contact details on to one of the local officers and they'll contact you regarding this as soon as possible.'

Ten days later, PC Bored Voice calls me about the despicable crime to arrange a time he can come round and drink my tea.

We settle on 11am the next day and sure enough, at *1.15pm*, he turns up and proceeds to take a statement, eating me out of Jaffa Cakes as he does so.

As this is just about a wing mirror being kicked off a car, I'm rather surprised that it takes over an hour for the statement to be completed.

PC Bored Voice has to fill out at least three separate forms, as well as taking several minutes to hand over a series of pamphlets to me which detail what organisations exist to help me deal with the severe trauma I've suffered as a victim of crime.

This incident isn't up there with evil garden gnome theft, but he's still required to sift through several badly printed brochures plastered with stock pictures of well meaning social workers, just in case I'm now too traumatised to function in polite society.

If you're lucky enough not to live in Britain you'll probably need filling in a bit on how our police force operates - and why it's no doubt worse than yours.

For instance, you'd be forgiven for thinking that the British government was run by a bunch of criminals, judging by the amount of roadblocks they put in the way of efficient policing. It's frankly a wonder anyone gets brought to justice.

…politicians *are* a bunch of criminals of course, but not because they're growing 300 skunk bushes in the downstairs toilet, or committing random acts of GBH outside The Dog and Pendulum on a Saturday night.

The main roadblock for the police forces of England and Wales is the paperwork.

British police officers have the unenviable task of being protectors of the public safety *and* administration secretaries, and I'm sure coppers won't mind me stating that admin is not one of their strong points…

Hours of their time are wasted slowly tapping out witness statements on a computer and attaching arrest reports to court files with treasury tags, when they should be out on the street arresting Billy Burglar as he jumps out of old Mrs Teapot's bathroom window, having liberated her of the entire collection of priceless gold thimbles she's been hoarding for the past five decades.

A copper I know confided in me that he'd recently been the officer in charge of a pedal cycle theft from outside the local Morrisons. Looking on the computer system, *seventeen* separate working sheets, statements, reports and summaries had been logged. For the theft of a rusty BMX that was worth about tuppence.

Imagine how many there are for the average assault or robbery…

This level of pointless paperwork has been achieved because when placed in charge of anything British people are masters of the knee-jerk reaction.

Because the police were… ahem… a bit *lax* when it came to correct and proper investigation back in the eighties, the government decided the best way to tackle this problem was to mire all of them in so much paperwork that the chances of being casually racist or nonchalantly corrupt were reduced to zero.

Effective stuff, I'm sure you'd agree.

However, it also stopped the police from solving any *actual* crimes, which rather missed the point a tad.

———

This is all bad enough, but add the fact that police officers are forced to be *nice* to people these days and you have a real recipe for disaster.

Yes, once again - in their infinite wisdom - the edict came down from the government that police officers were not in fact guardians of justice, ready to deliver swift and uncompromising punishment to the villains in our streets. No, they were actually meant to be *'pro-active in engaging on a personal level with the community'* and *'sensitive to the feelings of the public when coming into contact with them during the course of their duties'*.

Ugh.

…no, actually.

That's not what coppers should be in my book - or anyone else who has half a brain cell.

The police should be *scary*.

Big, mean looking bastards that strike fear into the hearts of the criminal underbelly.

Unfortunately, it's a little hard to be scary when you're spending three hours at the local church parish meeting being harangued by pensioners about the youths who hang around the post office and vandalise the bus shelter.

Trying to make coppers *nice* is a hiding to nothing.

I don't care whether my local bobbies are taking my feelings into consideration when patrolling the streets, I just want them stepping on the windpipes of the little shits who are burgling all the houses down my street.

You can take all the community forums and public engagement events and shove 'em up your arse as far as I'm concerned. It's not what the police are for. They're thief takers, not bloody social workers.

Police Community Support Officers (or PCSOs) were brought in to increase the public's trust in the police and show how caring and sharing your local constabulary is.

PCSOs can't arrest anyone, have no power beyond an ordinary member of the public and are forced to wear a uniform partially plastered in a nice, friendly, and above all *unthreatening,* blue colour.

Of course they were actually introduced because some money minded genius up at the Home Office thought paying people ten grand less a year and sticking them out on the street with roughly the same power and clout as a new born baby was a better idea than training more coppers.

…bloody hell.

The practical upshot of all this is that *no-one* finds the police a scary or serious proposition anymore, including the hardened criminals out there who are no doubt having a good old laugh about the whole thing.

Damn!

Forgot to mention the other element introduced during the pussification of the police force in Britain by the New Labour government: the CPS - or Crown Prosecution Service to give them their full title.

You see, once upon a time, the police would catch a criminal, charge him with a crime - having gathered enough evidence - and would be an integral part of the criminal justice process, all the way through to gaining a conviction against the guilty scoundrel.

Not any more though... oh no.

Now the police catch a criminal, gather the evidence... and hand it over to a bunch of civilian administrators, who wouldn't know a violent offender if he stamped all over their flower beds and ate their dog.

The Completely Pointless Service (see what I did there?) now decide on what to charge an offender with and how long a sentence to go for should the case come to trial.

Sadly, as the CPS seems to be almost exclusively populated by social workers and liberal do-gooders, most rapists, drug dealers and general scum bags can look forward to a twelve month sentence - suspended for 10 years provided they promise not to murder anyone or burn down more than two houses a month.

To sum up:

In the UK you now have coppers who have to worry about equality, diversity and equal opportunities every second of the day, rather than enforcing the law and terrifying the local criminal element into submission

Even if they do by some miracle have time to arrest and charge someone, they immediately have to hand the job over to vegetarian Tracy and her CPS friends, who'll just set the scallywag free because *'their mummy didn't love them and they've been punished enough already, you big nasty policeman'*.

If you want to picture a police officer in Britain today, fix the image of a large angry bull dog in your mind...

... then put lipstick on it and dress it in a nappy.

Needless to say, the scallywag who vandalised my car was never caught and I never heard from PC Bored Voice again.

As we speak he's probably on a week long course teaching him how to be nice to ethnic minorities and puppies. My wing mirror had no hope.

At this juncture, you may be thinking something along these lines:

'Hang on a bleeding minute, Spalding. Where do you get off having opinions about the police force? What do you know about it?'

What indeed!

Well, I'm allowed to moan incessantly about the state of the force because I used to *be* a copper...

Not a full time one, mind you. I could never have hacked the paperwork.

I was in fact a Special Constable with my local force for five years.

The Special Constabulary is a fine institution, as old as the police force in its entirety, and consisting of volunteer police officers who give up their free time to help their regular colleagues, bolstering the ranks of lawmakers country-wide.

I became a 'Special' for the plain and simple reason that I didn't have the money or physique to be Batman.

That and the fact I grew up in a pretty rough area, where I'd seen first hand the kind of misery crime in all its facets can cause to a local community and decided to do something about it.

The straw that broke the camel's back was when an eighty three year old woman down the road from me was burgled and beaten to within an inch of her life by a piece of human filth. He stole her purse, which contained precisely three pounds and sixty two pence.

I went in to the local station the next day to ask for the joining forms.

I'm not pretending to be any kind of upstanding hero here, but you should know by now that I can get quite angry when provoked... and I always like to find a positive outlet for that anger when I can.

Hence joining the Specials.

...looking big and tough in the stab vest was just a happy bonus.
Honestly.

Being a police officer in a leafy English suburb like the one I live in now means you're never likely to have many dealings with the hardened criminal element.

Most of my duties consisted of confiscating alcohol from surly teenagers and attending community events where the local pensioners would berate me for not doing enough to stop the bus shelters getting vandalised.

I never had to do much paperwork, thanks to the miracle of the 'hand-over' to my regular colleagues, wherein I would get all the fun of nicking burglars and brawling with the local piss heads outside The Dog And Pendulum on a Saturday night, without having to worry about all the tedious filing that comes afterwards.

Which is fair enough considering Specials don't get paid a bean for their efforts, I think.

Every now and again, if I was very lucky, I would get 'tucked up' in a job worthy of a particularly exciting episode of The Bill.

The occasion an armed robbery happened less than two miles from where me and my mate Adi had bunked off for a quick smoke for instance…

It transpired that two balaclava clad scoundrels had accosted the owner of a local hairdressing salon and robbed him of his takings to the tune of five thousand pounds. They'd done this carrying a crow bar and a hatchet, which was a pretty unpleasant way to conduct business.

The call came over the radio and Adi and I hastily 'moved towards'.

…as hastily as two Special Constables with no permission to go over the speed limit or use the sirens could anyway…

By the time we arrived on scene the armed robbers had legged it… and the hunt was on!

While the paid regular officers got to whizz around in their swanky BMWs with the blues and twos going like the clappers, me and Adi had to go and search some nearby fields. These had absolutely no prospect of hiding any desperate armed criminals… but might contain an angry bull or two.

It was dark by this time, so off we scampered with our torches to see if we could discover anything interesting in the cold muddy field…

No armed criminals and no bulls thankfully.

However, just as we're about to give the whole thing up as a waste of time, the police helicopter arrived overhead.

My ranting diatribe about the pussification of the police force aside, I'd like to think the constabulary is still competent most of the time, able to cope with the rising tide of crime in the UK (just about) and protect us all from the anti-social teenagers and mouth breathing rapists.

However, in the interests of complete transparency I am duty bound to recount the conversation that took place over the police radio at this point - to highlight the fact that even the police don't get things right all the time:

Helicopter: 'Tango 99 to India Lima 58…'

India Lima 58 (the Inspector on the ground near us): 'Go ahead, 99.'

Tango 99: 'I can see heat signatures in the field near you, 58. Might be our suspects.'

India Lima 58: 'Roger. Will call Bravo Mike 63 (the dog unit) to search.'

Spalding: 'Delta Bravo 76 to Tango 99… That's us, pilot. Stand dog unit down.'

Tango 99: 'Received 76, where are you?'

Spalding: 'Er… I'm in the field. Like I just said.'

Tango 99: 'Exactly where 76?'

Spalding: 'In the middle, I guess. I'm standing near a little shed. It's got a red roof.'

Tango 99: 'My camera is black and white 76. Can you identify yourself?'

Spalding: 'I could jump and down a bit if you like.'

Tango 99: 'Roger that 76.'

Spalding: 'I'm jumping up and down now.' (gasping for air) 'Oh shit, I've dropped my torch.'

Tango 99: 'Roger that 76. There's another heat signature at the back of the field. Bravo Mike 63, can you investigate?'

Bravo Mike 63: 'Roger that. Am in field now.'

Adi: 'Stand down Bravo Mike 63, that's me. I'm stuck on some barbed wire.'

Bravo Mike 63: 'Roger that. Where are you? Near the little shed?'

Adi: 'Negative 63. Am at rear of field.'

Bravo Mike 63: 'Roger that. Will take dog to centre of field to investigate other heat signature near little shed.'

India Lima 58: (Cutting across everyone else so the dog unit can't hear the helicopter saying it's me in the middle of the field) 'How many heat signatures do you have 99?'

Tango 99: 'Three.'

Bravo Mike 63: (Having seen my shadow in the gloom) 'Possible suspect sighted in field, am releasing dog.'

Spalding: 'Aaarrgghh!! That's me 63! That's me! Stand down! Stand down!'

Bravo Mike 63: 'Roxy! No! No! Get back!'

Tango 99: 'Everything alright 76?'

Spalding: 'Roger 99. Anyone have a change of underwear on them?'

Yes indeed… your local constabulary working in perfect harmony there, folks.

While this farce was playing out to an audience of one befuddled cow, the armed robbers were being collared outside the Budgens in the High Street, having neglected to provide themselves with a suitable get away vehicle.

They were both seventeen, semi-illiterate and were on twelve month suspended sentences for other crimes.

I hope Tony Blair reads this.

…and David Cameron for that matter. I'm deathly afraid he's just Tony Blair wearing an unconvincing rubber mask and will not be persuaded otherwise until he disbands the CPS.

Even the prospect of getting my wedding tackle bitten off by an enraged dog - for the second time in my life - doesn't go down as the most embarrassing episode in my career as a Special Constable.

That particular award goes to an incident a mere three months before I had to give up the voluntary police work due to the day job getting busier and demanding too much of my time.

Adi and I (we tended to team up a lot. It was like Starsky & Hutch without the cardigans and excitement) arrived at a domestic violence job in one of the less savoury local neighbourhoods.

It appears the woman of the house - a nineteen stone behemoth covered in tattoos, was abusing her ten stone husband - a small man who faintly resembled a weasel.

It looks like the latest argument had resulted in her accosting him with a rolling pin, splitting his skull open like a grapefruit.

The behemoth was arrested by our regular colleagues, but as she was 'well known' to police as a drug dealer, Adi and I were tasked to search the house for any narcotics around the place that we could additionally nick her for.

Time for a requisite Spalding aside:

The police force has a never-ending revolving door policy when it comes to its senior staff.

Chief Inspectors, Superintendents and Chief Superintendents come and go like the seasons as they all shuffle round one another trying to justify their inflated pay packets.

We'd recently obtained a new Chief Superintendent in our operational policing area - or 'OPA' as it was called. The police have never met an acronym they didn't like.

He was a tall, rangy fellow with a craggy face like Beachy Head and the shortest, sharpest haircut you've ever seen.

We'll call him Chief Superintendent Overpaid for the purposes of this story.

CS Overpaid was one of those pro-active types who wanted people to think he was 'part of the team' and 'first amongst equals'.

This was epic bullshit of course and nobody believed a word of it.

As part of his campaign to get to know the troops and patronise them, CS Overpaid had decided to come out on shift with the local patrol team to see what crime was like in the area. The night Adi and I went to the domestic was also the night he had chosen to do this.

Keep this in mind as the following story unfolds.

So we're in behemoth's bedroom.

The room is, shall we say, *fragrant* to say the least.

A sweaty haze hangs in the air and there's mould growing on stuff that's disgusting enough for me to be very glad there's mould growing all over it so I can't see what it is.

The bed looks like it hasn't been made since it was bought and the wallpaper is peeling off the damp walls in long strips.

Sounds delightful, doesn't it?

Have a chat with a copper sometime, I bet they can describe worse.

We've conducted a search of most of the bedroom – mainly with our eyes it has to be said, neither of us have had our shots – and the only thing left to investigate is the large wooden cupboard tucked in the corner.

'You open it,' Adi says.

'Fuck off, there could be anything in there,' I reply.

'I know. That's why you should open it.'

'I have a son, you know.'

'Two sons, one daughter. Open the fucking cupboard Spalding.'

Having lost the 'I've got more to live for than you' competition I reach out a tentative hand and close shaking fingers round the handle.

Shielding my face with my free hand, I pull the door open.

What greets our dumbfounded eyes is the most complete collection of sex aids I've ever seen in my life.

You know in action movies when the hero goes to his massive wall of guns to select an appropriate level of firepower to deal with the dastardly drugs baron that's recently killed his pet dog?

Replace all those sleek black machine guns and pistols with equally sleek black vibrators and dildos and you've just about got the right mental image.

It was a cornucopia of equipment any branch of Ann Summers would have been proud to stock:

Butt plugs, love beads, cock rings, whips, chains, vibes, mega-size tubes of lube… and what looked like something you'd clean your fish tank with.

Adi and I reacted in the manner you'd expect. We laughed our arses off.

Levels of hilarity only increased when he picked up a string of love beads and hung them round his neck, performing a surprisingly accurate impression of Marge Simpson.

Not wanting to let Adi be the last word in sex toy related mirth I picked up what looked like the single longest dildo in existence. It was bright pink, at least three feet long and terminated in an enormous rubber cock at both ends.

I wrapped the double ender round my head and pretended it was a snake attacking me.

Adi was now laughing so hard tears were streaming down his face. He actually snorted like a pig.

'Snakes! Why did it have to be snakes!' I cry, doing my best Indiana Jones.

Having exhausted the entertainment possibilities of dildo-as-killer-snake, I move on to putting the monster between my legs - and proceed to poke Adi in the arse with it. I accompany this with a horrific falsetto female voice: *'Come on big boy! You know you want a good shafting, you naughty little fucker!'*

In my hysterical state, with one hand grasping the three foot double cock, the other held aloft in the air in as camp a gesture as I can generate, I turn round to see Chief Superintendent Overpaid standing in the doorway with my sergeant.

He's decided a visit to the serious domestic incident he'd heard about over the radio would be a good way of bonding with his new officers.

Hilarity turns to sheer, unbridled horror.

Ironically enough, Adi looks like somebody has in fact just rammed a three foot dildo up his arse.

I drop the monster, and in mind-bending fear and confusion I stand to attention.

Nobody stands to attention in the police force.

Nobody is ever *required* to stand to attention in the police force.

It's only done in the armed forces, so why I chose to do it now is beyond me to this day. It's a bloody miracle I didn't snap off a fucking salute.

'What the hell are you two idiots doing?' screams the sarge, going a disturbing shade or red.

'Not taking their job altogether seriously,' says Overpaid in a calm voice, a slight smile threatening to appear on his face.

The next few minutes were spent spouting profuse apologies – something I've become very good at over the years.

Luckily for Adi and me, Overpaid had a sense of humour, otherwise I might be writing this book in a cell somewhere.

We do both receive an unofficial reprimand for our actions from the area Inspector about a week later though - a perfectly understandable response in the circumstances.

I thought the resulting nick names were quite creative for the most part.

I became 'Spaldildo' and Adi, who was only five foot five, became 'PC Pocket Cock'.

I took to hiding my notebook whenever I came into the station for fear of having pictures of gigantic vibrating phalluses drawn all over it.

I'm glad to have provided a degree of levity to my overworked and underpaid colleagues.

The bastards.

So even when Spalding is in a position of considerable responsibility, he can still make an idiot of himself.

I've resigned myself to this fact and have created various coping mechanisms to deal with it.

My decision to leave the Special Constabulary wasn't influenced by that mortifying incident, believe it or not.

I literally just ran out of time to do it - what with work, my son and a rapidly failing marriage.

I thoroughly enjoyed my time with the police force though and if you'll allow me to be serious for the briefest of moments: they do a very difficult job, dealing with some truly horrific people on a regular basis and don't really get the credit they deserve a lot of the time.

The media like to use the police as a whipping boy because they know it sells papers, but once in a while it'd be nice for someone to acknowledge what they do in a positive light.

...I'm talking about the frontline PCs and PCSOs here obviously.

The coppers with crowns and laurels on their shoulders - who sit behind desks all day planning meetings with one another - couldn't organise a piss up in a brewery if their lives depended on it.

Well there you go!

Our captain - a man of smooth voice and perfectly trimmed moustache - has just come over the tannoy to announce that we are approaching Sydney and will be landing very shortly, thus bringing this flight – and the first half of the book – to an end.

I'll have to switch off the laptop shortly if I'm to avoid incurring the wrath of the fat stewardess, but I've got a couple of minutes left to sum things up so far.

How was the flight for you?

I'm not too bad, I think…

My eyes are very heavy from lack of sleep though, and I have one of those dull headaches that squats at the back of your head, refusing to shift until you've drunk a pint of water and got seven hours shut eye.

It has to be said, writing is a very productive way of making a flight go quicker. When you get into your stride it's quite easy for hours to pass unnoticed.

I've probably annoyed the handful of passengers in the cabin with me because of the incessant tapping on the keyboard, but if they have been angered by it I haven't noticed… lost as I've been in a whirlwind of creative ecstasy.

You're looking quite spry, I'd say. Not too tired at all.

…livelier than me it has to be said.

I'm going to pretend it's *not* because you nodded off after we left Bangkok.

I know I got a bit political back there for a while, but you could have registered your distaste in a slightly more constructive manner. The snores were rather off putting.

You might want to tidy up the empty peanut packets that now litter your booth before fatso comes back and berates you for it.

Buckle your belt as well, I can feel the plane starting to drop and there's bound to be a little turbulence with the rising heat of the Australian outback to contend with.

This is where we part company for a while, my friend.

I'll see you in about a week, after I've attended far too many meetings and drunk far too much instant coffee.

It should be a fun visit though and I hopefully won't embarrass myself too much.

Alastair will bloody kill me if I don't make a good impression with the owners of this sports company, so I must be on my best behaviour.

I'm more than a little nervous about the whole thing, if the truth be told - and this conversation with you has done a lot to take my mind off it.

So once again thank you for your company!

It's always much appreciated.

Okay then... this is Spalding signing off for now and looking forward to his Australia trip.

Let's hope the weather is nice and sunny!

The Flight to the UK

Oh, alright… sun *burn*.

The weather was indeed nice and sunny as it turned out. A little *too* nice and sunny.

While I spent most of my time in air conditioned buildings looking at mind numbing PowerPoint presentations and equally boring flip charts, I did get some time to enjoy Sydney and the Central Coast.

I say 'enjoy'. What I mean is 'get burned to a crisp'.

I made the mistake every moronic British person does when they visit a hot country:

'Woo hoo! It's sunny! I don't have to wear three jumpers! I can walk around in hardly any clothes! Fantastic!'

Sizzle…

It wouldn't be so bad, but I was only in Oz on holiday last year, up in Cairns. I should have learned my lesson then. You don't go out without Factor 10000 slapped all over your body and a big sun hat parked on your noggin.

For the last few days though I've been blissfully cavalier about my attitude towards sun protection and I'm now paying a hefty price.

I can only put this lapse in common sense down to the fact that I've been ostensibly 'at work' and things like sun cream and floppy hats haven't really crossed my mind.

You're in a different frame of mind when you're on holiday and more attuned to such considerations.

Also, Sydney is a lot further south, so the sun shouldn't be as hot, right?

Wrong.

As we speak, I have sun burn goggles.

Most of my face is a rather hectic red, but for the two circles of pale British flesh around both eyes. They're exactly the same shape as my sunglasses, needless to say.

I fell asleep on my hotel balcony with my shades on and t-shirt off, and Captain Shiny Fireball assaulted me for a good thirty minutes before I woke up and ran inside hissing in pain like a hypochondriac vampire.

I've been wearing the shades as much as possible to try and hide my stupidity, but you're not allowed to keep them on as you go through customs, so I'm sure the entire crew of security officers in the terminal got a good laugh at the idiotic Brit as I passed through.

...at least it detracted from the horror of my passport photo.

I wore the sunglasses onto the plane, but have removed them now, as sitting in Business Class with shades on makes me look like an utter twat - or 'rock musician' if you prefer.

Apart from the face burn, every time I shift in my seat my t-shirt scrapes across my crispy shoulder blades, causing me to wince and wish I'd spent the last few days in Norway.

I would take the shirt off, but I covered myself in so much after sun lotion at the hotel before I left, I fear I may slide off the chair like a pig on a greased ramp and head butt the TV in front of me.

If I did this I wouldn't even be able to sue, as I'm on a Qantas flight on the way back, rather than British Airways.

The Australians haven't as yet caught the litigious health and safety disease our country suffers from, so I probably wouldn't get a brass farthing out of them.

This is actually one of the reasons why I love the country and would emigrate there at the first opportunity...

What a *fantastic* place Australia is.

It's just like the UK - only with sunshine and hope.

And if you do something stupid over here - like get hideously sun burned - you've only got yourself to blame.

How refreshing is that?

To live in a country that doesn't pander to the lowest common denominator?

The nanny state mentality that permeates Britain hasn't infected the Antipodes and doesn't look likely to any time in the near future, either. This is just as well, as there's so much stuff over there that can kill you in a variety of interesting and painful ways, the law suits and legal proceedings would clog up the courts system for the next thousand years, if their attitude was different.

We've got less killer spiders in the UK, but more morons. Our courts should be freed up in about five hundred years with any luck.

This is why criminals in Britain are getting away with murder...

If courtroom three is permanently full of mouth breathers trying to sue McDonalds for criminal negligence because they burned their lips on a hot apple pie, the chances of Billy Burglar getting the proper grilling he deserves from a jury of his peers are slim to none.

When you've got a justice system staggering under the weight of a thousand trumped up accident liability cases, is it any wonder there's a revolving door policy operating when it comes to petty - and not so petty - crime?

Much easier to give the drunken louts and anti-social gits a quick slap on the wrist, rather than try to build a strong case against them. That's far too time consuming...

Thanks Tony!

I really do hate that man.

Have you noticed?

When Nanny Tony got into power back in the late nineties he decided we were all too fragile and incompetent in the UK to take care of ourselves and set about removing as much personal responsibility from the populace as was humanly possible.

The Health & Safety monster started to rear its ugly head and instead of people having to think before engaging in a stupid act - like jumping out of a second story hotel window - they just went ahead and did it anyway, safe in the knowledge they'd be able to sue the hotel for negligently not spot-welding the windows shut on every floor except the ground.

What all that health and safety legislation we have to suffer with fails to take into account is that human beings are endemically idiots.

You won't stop people doing stupid things by plastering posters everywhere and wrapping anything with a point in bubble wrap.

You *will* create a nation of feckless drones however, who all think Nanny Tony will be there to pick them up and dust them down no matter how stupidly they act.

Tony and his government also made the unforgivable mistake of thinking everyone was equal and therefore deserved equal treatment.

This is of course *horseshit*.

Everyone is different.

You can tell that just by looking at people's faces.

Try to treat everyone the same and all you do is spread yourself way too thin, providing an adequate service to no-one.

Case in point: Student fees.

When I was a lad, getting into university was a privilege, not a right. You actually had to *study*, pass a series of exams and get high enough grades to gain entry to the higher educational establishment of your choice.

Because of this, less people went to university.

Not everyone was smart enough and the ones who didn't pass the exams had to go off and find a job instead.

Less students meant less strain on the budgets and those who were clever enough to get in, but not rich enough to support themselves, were given grants to assist with their education and living expenses.

Fast forward to Nanny Tony's government and now everyone *deserves* to go to university, right?

RIGHT?!

Everyone is equal!

Everyone should have the same opportunity to do a pointless media degree… not just those poncy smart kids.

Admission standards slipped, student numbers went up and budgets rose to compensate.

Suddenly there was no money for grants, and students had to be charged for their education.

So while even dumb people got to study a degree, the odds of *anyone* finishing their course without being thousands of pounds in debt were lower than Gordon Brown's charisma.

And because there were many more lovely graduates out there, the chances of finding a job dropped dramatically as well, such was the increase in competition.

Thanks Tony!

Don't even get me started on the benefits system…

In their admirable desire to make sure everyone in need got the benefits they rightfully deserved, the New Labour government forgot that while a lot of people do indeed deserve them, there are also a lot of scumbags out there who will abuse the system at every given opportunity unless you keep a tight bloody rein on proceedings.

The government didn't do this of course, placing a disproportionate amount of trust in the public to only claim what they honestly needed.

Hah!

This represented a frightening lack of common sense that has led to millions being handed out to lazy, selfish bastards - none of whom have any sense of personal responsibility or morality, and quite happily pirate movies and throw themselves off hotel balconies on a regular basis.

The thousands of poor sods who actually need the help are forgotten about as the welfare system stretches to breaking point due to the cheats that don't deserve a hand out.

If you're going to run a benefits system properly – and arguably a country – you've got to do it with a healthy dose of cynicism.

Note to future politicians: Treat everyone as a dick until proven otherwise and you might do a halfway decent job.

———

The Health & Safety monster jumped out on me last year when I took Tom to a birthday party at one of those horrible children's adventure play parks.

It was a six year old boy's idea of paradise, full of inflatable objects and padded obstacles, ready to be climbed over, jumped into and thrown up on.

Everything was great until a skinny teenager came forward holding some helmets.

Helmets.

Cast your peepers back three sentences. See the words 'inflatable' and 'padded' up there do you?

I thought as much.

You can imagine the look on my face when this pale eighteen year old girl extended a black coal scuttle-like helmet towards my robust, healthy son.

'Are you having a laugh?' I said.

'New rules I'm afraid sir,' paleface says in a monotone that suggests this isn't the first time she's had to explain.

'It's a bit ridiculous, isn't it?' I counter.

The mother of one of the other boys catches my attention. 'Don't bother Nick. It's been like this for months now, ever since two girls smacked their heads together jumping about. The parents sued.'

The parents *sued*.

Yes indeed, we live in a country where parents can send their children off to play in a big group on what amounts to a gigantic bouncy castle – and can then extort money out of the bouncy castle owners when one of the little darlings gets a bump on the head.

What's next, I wonder?

If I give Tom a box cutter and he severs a couple of fingers, can I sue Stanley?

If I stick my penis into a window frame and slam the PVC window on it, can I take Everest to court?

If I take it upon myself to run over my own head with the front wheel of my car, can I get a few bob out of BMW?

Because we don't want the idiots to sue, health and safety has now taken on epically stupid proportions.

Tom certainly agrees - and he still thinks Superman is real.

Off he trotted towards the play area, face like thunder and head covered in a helmet that made him look like one of the 'special' children.

He spent a lacklustre twenty minutes bouncing around with his similarly attired brethren before they all grew quite apathetic about the experience and came back for hot dogs.

The hot dogs were the microwaveable kind. On the side of the foil packet was the warning: CAUTION - FOOD MAY BE HOT.

I'm not quite sure who's to blame for all this, but I'm looking in your direction America…

For the sake of comparison, while in Queensland, Australia last year on holiday with Jenna, I rolled up in the hire car to a ferry that crossed one of the state's many picturesque, tropical rivers.

The safety measures designed to protect you from falling into the fast moving current and being eaten by one of the ravenous local crocodiles consisted of a single piece of rope tied to a series of skinny metal poles that ran down both sides of the ferry.

There was also a *tiny* yellow sign with a picture of a crocodile on it and the word 'dang' written in felt tip pen above. I assume it was supposed to say danger, but the last two letters had been rubbed off.

I got out of the car to stretch my legs a bit and noticed all of this.

Somewhat bemused, I walked over to the ferryman, who was a rather garrulous looking individual with a leathery face almost completely hidden from sight by an enormous beard. He sat on the rusty remains of a metal chair, smoking a roll-up and looking completely content with his world.

'Here mate,' I said, pointing to the largely inadequate safety precautions. 'What happens if somebody falls in, then?'

He smiled broadly. 'The crocs get a snack mate, that's what.'

'Yeah… but what I mean is, who gets the blame? Would you get in trouble?'

He looked at me quizzically. 'Why would I get in trouble?'

'Coz you're the ferryman. It's your ferry. You're in charge,' I said, hammering home the point as best I could.

'Look mate, if someone's dumb enough to get too close to the edge and falls in, that's their bloody problem, not mine. Some French fella went in a few years ago. Drunk, he was. We found his hat a few days later.'

'And no-one sued?'

'Sued? What the hell for? Bloke was a fucking idiot.'

I would have kissed him were it not for the disturbing amount of old food nestling in his beard and the fact he only appeared to have four teeth.

I know the Aussies have a reputation for being happy as pigs in shit because of the glorious weather they live in, but I'm bloody convinced it's also due to the fact they're a nation of people who still know the value of personal responsibility and expect people to not act like the mentally deficient all the time.

The tosspots that would otherwise bring their country down with their whining and benefits cheating have all been eaten by the plump and happy crocodiles.

Their immigration policy should be looked at *very* closely by the UK Home Office.

The Australians seem to think it's a good idea to only let people in who can prove they will benefit the economy and country as a whole.

This screws me royally if I ever want to emigrate out there, because trying to prove the value of being a marketing copywriter and author of comedy books involving public defecation and vomiting might be a tad on the tricky side.

The Aussies also tend to turn convicted criminals away at the border, working on the notion that they might not be the *best* type of person to be wandering along Bondi Beach of an afternoon.

In the official list of the best countries to live and work in, Oz is second and the UK languishes in twenty first, just above Slovenia, where they eat their own pets.

Makes you sick, doesn't it?

Having said all that, they're not *perfect*.

A couple of days ago I had the chance to see the delights of the Central Coast just north of Sydney and took the opportunity to pop up there to amble along the beach in my flip-flops.

A pleasurable past time only increased in enjoyment by being able to send a Facebook update via my phone to all my miserable, cold friends back home telling them exactly what I was doing.

Small aside:

This is the primary reason why Facebook is as popular as it is - in the UK at least.

Your man Zuckerberg will try to convince you it's because Facebook provides a valuable social network, where people from across the globe can communicate and form meaningful relationships.

Squirrel nuts, I say.

The truth is it succeeds because it's the quickest way to let everybody else know that you're having a better time than they are.

Nothing says *'Yeah... I'm richer, more successful and more popular than you, you nasty little troll,'* better than a Facebook profile stuffed to the gills with witty status updates about how the new car matches your eyes, and high resolution pictures of your last three holidays to the Expensive Islands.

While on my walk, I became aware that I was by far and away the ugliest person on the beach.

And the palest.

And the fattest.

It was like Poseidon himself had decided to have a clear out of all the hot bodied, sexually alluring people of Atlantis - throwing them unceremoniously up onto dry land to get rid of them.

I tried my hardest to only look at the dynamite girls, but my traitorous neuroses kept dragging my eyes back to the Adonis-like Australian men, as they jogged past on their way to do something worthwhile like save kittens from drowning or re-home some orphans probably.

Look at them, the blasted wasteland of my ego says. *Look how much better they are than you. Compare their six packs and chiselled pectorals to your dough-like body. Why aren't you walking round in a boiler suit so the perfect people don't have to look at you, you fat mess?*

Then one of them ran up to me…

'G'day!' he exclaims, smiling a smile of such toothy whiteness I feared for my eyesight.

'Morning,' I reply hesitantly.

From his tiny red swimming briefs he produces a card. I try not to dwell on where he might have been keeping it.

'My name's Brett and I'm the local environment agency rep. Just getting people's opinions on the cleanliness of the beach,' he tells me, removing his action packed sunglasses to reveal a set of deep blue eyes that every woman I've ever met would get instantly wet looking into. Shit, even I'm starting to get a *bit* horny.

…and this guy works for the environment agency!

Back in England, his equivalent is Trevor – a thirty six year old virgin with alopecia and a disturbing addiction to World Of Warcraft.

'Right…' I say, examining the card with his name and job title on.

It seems this guy's main responsibility is to run up and down the beach in his tiny red briefs asking people how much they love this particular corner of paradise.

I hate him with a passion that's almost holy.

'You British, mate?' he smiles.

I don't know whether to punch him or French kiss him.

This always happens to me.

You might have already read the tale of the American lizard in the Chanel suit I bumped into in Beverley Hills, but I could also tell you about the taxi driver in Mumbai and the prostitute in Oslo.

I'm not going to, as I might want to write a third one of these one day and need to hold some material back.

Suffice to say I seem to be a constant source of surprise and amusement to the locals of whatever nation I happen to stumble into.

'Yes I am,' I reply, trying to keep the exasperation out of my voice.

'That's great mate, you Poms are always good for a laugh.'

I don't know whether this is a compliment or an insult, but I'm not taking any chances.

'On vacation, are you?' he says, his perfectly tanned legs jogging up and down on the spot. They're being forced to do this as I've now ground to halt. It's bad enough standing still next to this ridiculous human being, I don't need to be jogging alongside him as well.

'Today I am. Here on business mainly though.'

'Nice. What d'you do?'

'I'm a copywriter.'

'A copywriter? Sounds bad mate.'

Well, that's charming. Brett's now critiquing my employment. 'What's wrong with that?'

'Indoor job, mate. *Indoor* job.' He says 'indoor' the same way you or I would say 'up to your neck in human faeces'.

'Yes, I suppose it is,' I accept and let out a gasp of breath, unaware I'd been holding my gut in since Brett rocked up.

'Couldn't do that, mate,' he says. 'Don't like air conditioning and offices. Don't know how you do it every day!' He gives me a friendly slap on the shoulder.

I am now so soul-destroyingly depressed I can barely look at the bastard. 'Well, it… it pays quite well,' I mutter feebly.

But *who cares* how much my disgusting 'indoor' job pays?

I'm not Brett - who calls the most beautiful beaches in the world his office and wears tiny red briefs instead of an ill-fitting grey suit.

I bet he doesn't have to slope over to the Co-op every lunch time for a low fat chicken salad sandwich and bruised apple, does he? I bet he doesn't stand around the water cooler every Monday morning discussing the X Factor and wishing he was dead. I bet he never missed the 'I' out of Public Services or shot a pharmaceutical giant with a paint ball on a god-awful team building weekend…

Aaarggh!

In resignation I look back at Brett, managing to keep the loathing out of my eyes. 'Well, your beach is very nice, Brett. Yes, your beach is very nice indeed.'

The smile returns to his face and I squint as the sun reflects off his even, white teeth. 'Bonza!'

Yes. He actually said *bonza*.

'See you, mate! Enjoy yourself!' Brett says by way of goodbye, and jogs off to rejoin the other perfect bodies as they tear up the beach.

101

Well, *thanks* Brett.

I was just starting to enjoy myself and then you come along and remind me I'm not you, you utter perfect bastard...

I tried to make myself feel better by copying Brett and jogging along the beach.

It didn't work.

I burned my feet on the sand and pulled a muscle.

I started this anecdote off saying not all Australians are perfect... but they are damn them! And Brett is the zenith of this perfection.

I can usually do a good job of hiding towering jealousy, but when it comes to the bloody Australians I just can't. They live in paradise, look fantastic, have a booming economy, are endlessly happy, refreshingly friendly and have a 'fair go' attitude that the rest of the world could sorely do with adopting.

I think this is the first case in human history of a man wanting to have sex with an entire country.

Countryphiliac?

Nymphomainlandiac?

8.23pm EST
33510 Words
Over Indonesia. Someone tried to sell me a fake iPhone from there the other day. I declined.

Oh god… did you hear that?

The sound I made when I sat back in the seat?

'Hurrgh.'

That's what it sounded like: *Hurrgh.*

If there was ever a sure sign of getting older it's making noises when you sit down or get up.

It's like your body's been doing it for so long now it's bored of making the same old movement and wants you to know about it.

I'm not claiming to be falling into my dotage at the grand old age of thirty eight or anything, but I'm certainly starting to notice changes in myself that I can only attribute to the fact I'm getting closer to the 'magic' age of forty.

Along with the getting out of chair noises and the rapidly decreasing mobility in my left knee, I've noticed a new found propensity for tutting.

I never used to tut, unless it was in an ironic fashion.

Now though, I find myself genuinely tutting when I see something I disapprove of.

I figure the slow head shaking will kick in around forty five and my arms will naturally start folding when I hit fifty.

On a far, *far* more serious note, another problem I've encountered is the inability to maintain an erection. It's only happened once so far, but once was enough for Nick Spalding, thanks very much.

I'm hoping and praying it isn't a sign of things to come.

It happened last year and I truly thought the world had come to an end.

There are some mitigating circumstances, in my defence:

It had been years since my break-up with Sophie and I was very… *rusty.*

Add this to a rather bruised self esteem due to the divorce and I think the lack of standing to proper attention is partially forgivable.

…I still mainly put it down to the aging monster though.

I've been through many periods of stress, unhappiness and worry in my life, but little Spalding had previously never failed to do his duty during any of them.

This horrific failure to launch happened the first time Jenna and I got 'jiggy wid it' - to quote Will Smith.

Some three weeks into our burgeoning relationship we went for a meal at a picturesque Italian restaurant just off the beaten track.

It was at the back of both our minds that this would be the night to consummate things. We'd progressed naturally through the stages of dating to the point at which sex was definitely on the cards (there was nowhere else to go really. The previous date had ended with dry humping on the bonnet of her car).

Both of us were dressed for the occasion.

She wore a gorgeous pale blue blouse and pencil skirt (with extremely sexy but uncomfortable stockings and suspenders underneath, I was later to discover) and I wore my best dark blue jeans and grey cashmere sweater.

I even wore a pair of boxer shorts that didn't have any holes around the crotch, which *really* proves I was making an effort.

The date went well, despite me ordering a pizza slathered with anchovies and onion (thank the lord for Smints) and her nearly choking on a particularly large green olive.

We had a lovely conversation over the wine and non alcoholic beer, but we were out of the restaurant by half past nine… as we both knew what we'd rather be doing.

Back at my house, I barely get to the kitchen to boil the kettle for a cuppa before Jenna is putting her arms around my shoulders and moving in for the kill.

Now, I could get pornographic here…

But much like the story featuring the loss of my virginity in the last book, I will steer clear of lurid descriptions, as it isn't the point of the story.

Also, I'd like to keep my relationship with Jenna on the right track if it's all the same to you. Five graphic paragraphs detailing our first sexual liaison would *not* be the best way to accomplish this.

…please stop looking so disappointed, it makes me feel bad.

Suffice to say, twenty minutes later sees us both in the bedroom divested of a majority of our clothing.

At this point Spalding Jnr is behaving in an appropriate manner and I could have hung towels off him if I'd wanted to.

Have I mentioned the fact I was up at 6am that day?

No, I'm sure I haven't…

At the age of twenty seven this would have mattered not a jot. At the age of *thirty* seven, things are quite different.

Inexplicably, as Jenna is busy kissing my chest in a *very* pleasant way, I let out a yawn…. barely stifling it before her head comes up for a kiss.

Shit… that's not good.

I can't let her see me yawn. How embarrassing would that be for both of us?

So now, instead of concentrating on the soft feel of her lips as they roam over my body, I'm thinking about not yawning.

Have you ever tried to not yawn? It's bloody hard.

Also, stifling a yawn inexplicably makes you feel *more tired*. Suppressing the reflex action turns the tiredness in on itself somehow. I'm not a medical person so I don't know if there's a fancy term for this, but it's an annoying phenomenon of the human body either way.

Another traitorous urge to yawn hits me and I stifle it again, making an expression like I'm holding in a fart.

Jenna notices it this time.

'Are you ok?' she asks.

This is not the kind of thing you want a woman to say at any time during love making. Especially when it's your first time with her.

'Yeah, yeah, I'm fine,' I lie.

But I'm not, because I've spent so much time fretting about the yawning thing I've forgotten what I'm here for and little Spalding is starting to wilt.

I'm not worried about yawning anymore.

A far bigger problem has reared its ugly head:

I'm losing my stiffy!

Now my undivided attention is devoted to thinking about as many sexy things as I can to prevent my winky going soft.

I concentrate on the way Jenna's breasts are rubbing across my chest.

I think about the fabulously sexy black underwear and stockings she's wearing.

I replay the last porno I watched in my head that featured two lesbians in tiny pants.

I think about the spectacular blow job Hayley Morrison gave me at a wedding in 1993.

I ruminate on that time Sophie and I had sex in the New Forest on a gorgeous summer's day – a session that's still in my all time top ten.

Right now, as I'm writing this, all those memories are going through my head and I'm starting to get a bit horny. I'm sat in a business class seat on a plane somewhere over South East Asia, without a woman in sight, and I can feel definite *stirrings*.

The same could not be said for last year in my bedroom, as a hot, semi-naked woman played with my balls.

Little Spalding had surrendered.

Given up the ghost... packed it in... taken a powder... quit the match and gone off to the showers.

Oh, the *horror*.

Jenna stops fondling me as she realises something's gone very wrong and gives me a quizzical look.

I start to spout apologies.

She asks if it's her… and I tell her over and over again that it isn't.

And it really wasn't!

The problem is all me - due to a hellish concoction of nerves, being out of practise and the big lumbering bastard of being in your late thirties.

I'm used to relaying incidents in my life that were quite embarrassing, but this is the only one that still makes my face go red as I write it down.

Maybe that's because it didn't happen all that long ago.

I have no doubt it's also down to the fact it was such a soul-destroying, excruciatingly humiliating moment in my life.

I'm led to believe that this is the way all men feel when this happens…

'Well, that's that relationship screwed before it got going,' I reflect, as Jenna slides off me and perches herself on the edge of the bed.

With shame and doubt hanging heavily in the air, she gets dressed and makes motions to leave.

I don't stop her, as I've already accepted I'm never going to see her again and will be back to wanking myself into insensibility in no time – if I can ever get the bloody thing up again.

We both traipse down the stairs, her in front carrying her jacket in her arms almost protectively, me bringing up the rear at a sloth-like pace as I try to process what's just happened.

…are you cringing right now?

Yes. Yes, I can see you are.

It's a horrible situation, isn't it?

We exchange cursory goodbyes at the front door and she makes her way back down the drive to her car.

Jenna doesn't look back as she jumps into the driver's seat and fires up the engine.

106

I close the front door without even attempting a last wave goodbye and return to my lounge, where I sit disconsolately on my couch wishing I'd never signed up for that stupid dating service.

What with it being the twenty first century and all, I send Jenna a text message that says something along the lines of:

I'll understand if you don't want to see me again. It was nice to meet you. xx

About half an hour later she responds:

I would like to see you again, if you'd like to see me?

Bless her... she still thinks it might have been her fault.

This makes me feel ten times worse.

Mind you, how great is she to still want to go out on another date after that?

It was probably too early to be sure, but that might well be the moment I started to fall in love with Jenna.

To see past our collective embarrassment and not let a mild case of impotence scare her off was a real sign of character.

I could hardly believe my luck, to be honest. To get a second chance after that disaster is like winning the lottery.

I was terrified the next time we tried to have sex, of course.

What if it happened again? What if I could never get a hard-on *ever* again??

Horrors!

Needless to say that didn't happen.

I may be dumb enough to write down every embarrassing thing that happens to me and publish it for the world to read, but I'm not likely to announce that I'm permanently impotent. You have to draw a line in the sand somewhere.

A few days later I found myself in Jenna's flat, heart racing and expecting the worst.

With a little encouragement from her - and acknowledgement that I was a very scared thirty seven year old boy – things went more according to plan.

I won't say it was the most astronomic sex in history. Far from it.

I still fumbled around and it was over in a time scale usually reserved for the process of boiling an egg, but it did come to a fairly satisfactory climax and my sense of self worth was restored.

By the time we reached our fifth shag I was back to being the legendary swordsman of my youth (hah!) and the disgrace of the night when the floppy fairy came to visit was almost forgotten.

Over the past year I've made every effort to make up for those first few fumbling sexual encounters with Jenna.

She's still with me, so I guess I must have done a good job of it.

Silver lining time:

When you do reach your late thirties it might be more difficult to get it up if you're feeling stressed, anxious or tired, but once it *is* standing to attention properly and you're nice and relaxed... you can hump for hours. Premature ejaculation is no longer a problem.

Yippee!!

That's the most extreme example I can give of how the march towards forty is affecting me.

I could spend another unhealthy five thousand words on all the other ways, but I want to keep you smiling, not thinking about slitting your wrists, so I'll resist the temptation.

Anyway, it's not all bad.

There are also a lot of benefits to getting older:

Not giving a fuck what anyone thinks about you is great.

You spend your teens and twenties in a constant state of terror that you're not popular / successful / good looking / sexy / intelligent / brave enough, but by the time you hit thirty five that state of terror has turned into one of complete indifference. There are maybe – *maybe* - six people in this world whose opinions I now care about. I don't give a flying squirrel what the other six billion people on this planet think of me. This is extremely liberating and means I'm now more fun at parties.

Having quite a bit of money.

If you've been lucky enough to get a decent job and haven't made any silly mistakes, the chances are you've reached a point in your mid to late thirties when you've saved a few bob and can afford to go on expensive holidays to exotic locales. Backpacking around the Orient when you're nineteen and penniless *sounds* like a great idea - until the dysentery and herpes kick in, that is. I personally prefer having room service, a hire car and the secure knowledge I'm not going to be sexually molested outside a bar somewhere in Cambodia.

Lower car insurance premiums.

My nineteen year old nephew told me the other day how much it costs for him to insure his Honda Civic. I nearly fell off my chair from laughing so hard.

Life experience.

Without which it's impossible to write two comedy autobiographical books. I could have attempted this kind of thing at the age of twenty three, but the book would have lasted two thousand words and mainly been about wanking.

As age does its hideous work of turning you into a wrinkled, impotent cynic, it's important to maintain a young frame of mind, to stave off the worst effects of the aging monster for as long as possible.

To whit:

Spalding's Top Ten Ways To Stay Young!

1. The total and complete avoidance of cardigan. There's no reason for you to ever wear a cardigan or anything *remotely* cardigan-like. Doing so is the first step on the slippery ramp that ends in a post mortem examination. If you ever find yourself in Marks & Spencer nodding in approval as you fiddle with an inch wide button attached to some cable knit, walk away immediately, buy some skinny jeans and download a My Chemical Romance album.

2. Make sure you go away for 'a dirty weekend' and not 'a trip to the country'. One involves lubricant and vibration, the other haemorrhoid cream and Parkinsons.

3. Be out of the house on a Sunday between the hours of 6pm and 9pm. This will ensure you won't catch one second of Antiques Roadshow, no matter what time the BBC choose to slot it into the listings. Exposure to this programme is fatal to your grip on rapidly diminishing youth. Before you know it you'll find yourself genuinely pleased for the wizened old crone when she finds out her thimble collection is worth three grand. I say 'wizened old crone', what I really mean is *you in five years*.

4. Keep listening to Radio One. I know a lot of it sounds terrible and that fat bloke in the morning is an arrogant prick, but treat it as a form of hypnotic suggestion. If you listen to it for long enough, all that youthful exuberance and hormonal stupidity is bound to sink in. **Never turn the dial to the left.** That way lies Radio Two - and madness.

5. Avoid anywhere that was fields when you were a lad.

6. Frequent masturbation is your friend. It proves that you still have what it takes, and that your virility levels are high, despite being alive before the internet was invented. Use the world wide web to find applicable material to assist you with this. If you don't know how to find porn on the internet, pay for one of those handy college courses - and bloody learn *Grandad*. Caveat: Don't masturbate so much that it leads to problems similar to the one I had above. Try to strike a happy medium.

7. I suppose I have to include something here about regular exercise and a healthy diet. How very annoying.

8. If you insist on getting your hair cut in the style of a celebrity, try to make sure it's one the newly trained hairdresser has actually *heard of*.

9. Drive fast. Everywhere you go. Yes it's scary, yes it might result in criminal proceedings and the extra expense of new tyres, but nothing says 'old fart' like pootling round at the speed limit everywhere you go, getting in the way of the prick behind you in the BMW with one wing mirror hanging off.

10. Remember the things that you loved when you were a kid and do/read/watch/listen to them every now and again. If you loved New Kids On The Block, then spin that CD up once a year and rock out to Hanging Tough. Watch Back To The Future and Flight Of The Navigator a couple of times. Go rollerblading with your friends and laugh your head off as the speed picks up. Be careful though eh? You don't want to throw your back out, you old bastard.

You can't fight getting old, but you can sure as hell go down swinging...

I know you're dying to ask:

What do you do to stay young, Spalding? What keeps you in touch with your inner sticky child?

…aside from the frequent masturbation, you mean?

I'm not sure whether it's advisable to admit this, but what the hell:

I read Batman comics, that's what.

…

Don't look at me like that.

…

No, seriously, stop it.

Sigh.

I'm going to have to justify myself here, aren't I?

A lot of my friends and colleagues thoroughly enjoy taking the piss out of me for liking a comic book character at the age of thirty eight. It probably can't hurt to spend a few paragraphs defending my position, in the hope it might shut them up for a while.

I love Batman.

Have done since I was the ripe old age of ten, and despite the vagaries and disappointments of adult life, I've never really grown out of my love for the mad, cape wearing lunatic.

I have a brushed aluminium Bat logo on my wall at home - the one from the new Chris Nolan films. This cost a bloody fortune.

The metal worker I had knock it out for me was slightly bemused about the whole thing, but did a fine job.

It's about three feet wide and takes pride of place above my mantelpiece. It's always a conversation starter when I invite people round.

Said conversation usually begins with something along the lines of: *'You're such a sad wanker, Spalding,'* but I take the insults and jibes with the good grace of someone who's heard it all a thousand times before.

I've got a Batman t –shirt on as I write this. It's one of The Joker actually. Heath Ledger R.I.P.

Like most people of my age, I first discovered the character via the wildly popular 1960s TV series starring Adam West.

It was always re-run on Channel 4 in the breakfast slot and I would get up extra early before school to watch it.

The garish colours, overblown characters, ridiculous plot devices and melodramatic cliff hangers all appealed to my ten year old brain immensely.

I'd happily trot off to school kapowing and kersplatting any offensive bushes that happened to get in my way, with that oh-so-catchy theme tune running round and round in my head until well into the first lesson of the day – which was usually maths, regrettably.

At that time I had no idea the funny man in the dodgy looking Batsuit was based on a character that came into being because his parents were brutally murdered right in front of him - at the same age I was when I watched the TV show.

I didn't discover the 'real' Batman until a couple of years later when, in a slightly misguided attempt to keep her son occupied, my mother purchased a Batman graphic novel that should only be read by adults. It was called 'The Dark Knight Returns' and it changed my life.

This Batman had nothing to do with Adam West…

The story is actually a parallel universe take on the Batman legend, focusing on a middle-aged Bruce Wayne. He comes out of retirement when Gotham City really starts going to the dogs, with gangs of criminals roaming the streets, terrorising the inhabitants and completely destroying the bus shelters.

Written by Frank Miller, the graphic novel is so dark it's almost pitch black, is ultra-violent, a diatribe on 1980s America, features a Batman who borders on being a fascist… and the greatest thing I'd ever read ever in the whole world ever, ever, *ever*.

Gone were the kerpows and kersplats.

Out the window was the Bat Shark Repellent and Bat Poles.

Replacing them was a six foot mentally unstable maniac who would only stop short of murder to prevent criminals from destroying the lives of innocent people.

His honour was untouchable, his strength of will was indomitable, his bravery was unquestionable… his ability to fuck people up was unbeatable.

As a boy whose dad was virtually absent from his life from the age of two (and he's only come back into it over the past decade... far too late to be any influence) I got the father figure I needed in the comic book character who patrolled the streets of Gotham under the shadow of night.

He wasn't the only one – I also fell in love with Indiana Jones, another upstanding hero who I could look up to. I always came back to the Bat nine times out of ten, though.

From the day I finished The Dark Knight Returns, I proceeded to devour every Batman story I could get my grubby little hands on. Especially the ones geared towards a mature audience that eschewed any cartoonish qualities.

I never liked Robin, and still don't.

I acknowledge he's an important part of the Batman mythos, but the idea of Bruce Wayne actively putting a small boy in harm's way when he went up against ruthless criminal nutcases like The Joker never rang true with my perception of Batman as an honourable, heroic individual.

The whole homosexual context to their relationship never occurred to me as a young boy, but as I grew older that element started to bother me more and more as well.

People defend Robin and his role in the Batman story, but for me he's an unfortunate holdover from a more innocent time, one that should really go by the wayside in today's complex and more cynical society.

...besides, he looks like a right fucking berk in those little green panties, doesn't he?

I read and re-read graphic novels like Arkham Asylum, The Long Halloween and Batman: Year One - which acts as a basis for Nolan's Batman Begins. I went through the entire back catalogue of comics, stretching back through the years as far as I could. My favourite was The Legends Of The Dark Knight, which featured serious stories - and no bloody Robin.

I guess my yearning for a decent father figure kept me coming back time and time again to stories about Batman's one man crusade against crime, and I'm not ashamed to say that a majority of the moral grounding I got through my early teens was due to Bruce Wayne's alter ego.

They're values I still hold dear to this day: Act honourably, protect those that need it, do all in your power to stop the bullies, cowards and other scum that blight the lives of people every day.

You might have thought I was joking when I said I joined the police because of Batman earlier... but I wasn't really.

Fictional comic book character he may be, but when you're an impressionable young boy, someone like Batman can fire your imagination and have a huge impact on how you live the rest of your life.

As I grew older my love for the character never died, but it did diminish somewhat as I grew up and discovered things like breasts and alcohol.

This is the natural way of things.

I stopped buying the comics – the ones I had went into the loft - and Batman became just another part of my childhood and nascent teenage years, along with Action Man, the World Wrestling Federation and the discovery of masturbation.

…none of which were connected I hasten to add.

I went and saw the old Batman movies in the eighties and nineties, needless to say.

The Tim Burton ultra-gothic ones weren't too bad, but the Joel Schumacher sequels were awful.

Neither filmmaker understood Batman as far as I was concerned.

Burton got closest with the first movie, but Schumacher was completely clueless, thinking the best way to depict Batman in the modern world was by aping the Adam West series with a massive budget and rampant homosexual imagery.

In 1997 Batman & Robin, starring George Clooney, effectively killed the character on screen, with its horrible neon aesthetic and performances from Schwarzenegger and pals that could only have been improved if they'd been given full frontal lobotomies before filming began.

I actually walked out of that movie halfway through. I've only ever done that three times in my life and one of the other two occasions was because I needed to throw up.

Then in early 2004, I read a rather interesting article on Aint It Cool News stating that the director of Memento (a film I still don't entirely understand despite watching it backwards *and* forwards), an unassuming British fellow called Christopher Nolan, was planning a new Batman movie about the character's early years.

Going under the moniker 'The Intimidation Game' it would star the weird bloke from American Psycho, Gary Oldman's moustache, Sir Michael Of Caine and Qui-Gon Jinn.

I profess I wasn't particularly interested…

Us Bat fans had been burned to a crisp by Schumacher's films and were very wary of anyone else attempting to bring Batsy back to the silver screen.

I dismissed the project, but decided I'd probably go and see it when it came out… only I wouldn't get my expectations up beforehand.

A few months later they released a picture of the new Batmobile.

I say Batmobile, I mean *Big Fucking Black Tank*.

Unlike the Big Fucking Yellow Waders, I loved it the first time I slapped eyes on it. It was cooler than a penguin with chilblains.

In fact, the vehicle looked a lot like the ridiculous battle wagon Batman drives round in throughout The Dark Knight Returns graphic novel.

I started to get more interested at this point.

Obviously Nolan was at least going for a look that was in keeping with the Batman I adored as a boy...

Roll on summer 2005 and the film - now titled Batman Begins - was released to the public in general, and Nick Spalding in specific.

I attended the multiplex with a mixture of trepidation, hope and contained excitement, accompanied by a mate who was also a Batman fan when he was a boy, though nowhere near as bad as me.

My reaction to the film?

I thought it was jolly good.

Jolly good indeed.

...

Oh alright, I *cried*.

Can you believe that? A thirty two year old man having a blub as he watches a movie about a man dressed in a rubber suit hitting people?

Well it's true.

Here's the reason why:

There's a moment in that film that stays with me to this day.

I can conjure it up in my mind whenever I want, along with the frisson of sheer boyhood delight that ran down my spine as it played across the cinema screen in front of me.

It's about halfway through the film and Bruce Wayne is out and about in Gotham for the first time as Batman.

He's tracked a drug dealing operation to the Gotham docks and is intent on stopping the criminals before they get away. In a maze of shipping containers, the gang go about their nefarious business until Batman steps in.

He proceeds to scare the living shit out of every one of them, whisking them one-by-one into the shadows where he beats them to a pulp.

This doesn't play out like a superhero movie – it's like watching a *horror* film, as the monster in the shadows systematically picks off the luckless victims.

Batman takes every gang member out and turns his attention to the leader, a man named Carmine Falcone.

Falcone is sat in his limousine, scared out of his wits. Holding a pistol, he utters the line *'What are you?'* in a terrified gasp, eyes darting everywhere looking for the unseen assailant.

The sunroof smashes, two enormous black arms come into the car, grab Falcone and pull him out.

With the music score building to a crescendo, Falcone faces the monster.

Squatting on the car roof like some horrific gargoyle, The Batman pulls Falcone to his masked face and whispers *'I'm Batman,'* before whisking the petrified gangster skywards.

That's when I cried…

For the first time it was *him* on screen.

The same man I'd read about as a boy.

The same man who I'd looked to in the absence of a father.

The same man who instilled in me a sense of honour I maintain to this day.

All at once he was right in front of me, thirty foot high and larger than life. Brought from the pages of the comic book and presented as something that existed in the real, moving world.

How could I not have felt that way?

…I stifled the sob of course.

I'd never have lived it down if my mate had seen or heard me bawling like a baby over my hot dog and bucket of Sprite.

The rest of the movie only got better.

Nolan and his team had obviously studied the comics well, capturing the character's essence perfectly. They treated Batman with complete respect for the first time ever outside the medium of comics.

This wasn't a camp superhero putting a stop to the schemes of a gallery of colourful, childish villains - nor was it a hyper-stylised depiction of the character warped out of all recognition by a filmmaker with his own agenda.

This was The Batman.

This was the character Bob Kane created in 1939, who has stayed in the public consciousness for over seventy years.

I left the cinema on a high - roughly the same height I'm at right now in this plane, I'd wager - and Nick Spalding aged ten stayed firmly in control of Nick Spalding aged thirty two for weeks afterwards.

I saw the film a further *three* times at the cinema with a variety of friends and relations.

As I write this I've seen it about twenty five times in total. No film has ever captured my imagination like it - with possible exception of Raiders Of The Lost Ark, because, well… it's Raiders Of The Lost Ark, isn't it?

Not even Indiana Jones's whip wielding adventure could compare to Batman Begins though.

…and then Nolan topped the bastard in 2008 with The Dark Knight.

———

I won't repeat all the plaudits that have been heaped on that film due to its realism (or *verisimilitude*, if you're a film studies student), epic storyline and brilliant performance by Heath Ledger - suffice to say there's one moment in it that made me cry as well, this time without being able to hide it successfully:

Towards the end, Batman enters a half constructed skyscraper to save a group of hostages taken by The Joker.

Police SWAT teams are also storming the building, but unknown to them the hostages have been dressed by The Joker as terrorists and vice versa – in a typically cunning move by the Clown Prince Of Crime.

Batman must take down the real terrorists *and* the SWAT teams to prevent any loss of innocent life.

Using an advanced sonar system - with Morgan Freeman's Lucius Fox updating him on the enemy's position via a radio link - Batman proceeds to take out *everyone* with customary precision.

Again the score by Hans Zimmer and James Newton Howard crescendos as the character works his magic, creating a visual and aural experience that's just fucking *Batman* to a tee as far as I'm concerned.

I blubbed like an idiot.

Luckily I was with my sister, so it wasn't all bad.

She only took the piss for a month or two…

Needless to say I'm looking forward to the third film in the trilogy 'The Dark Knight Rises' next year with slightly more excitement than the birth of my child.

I'll be at the cinema - front and centre - trying very hard not let anybody see me cry and hoping against hope that they haven't made the sodding thing in 3D.

I'm sure if you think about it, you can recollect forgotten joys from your childhood that elicit the same emotional reaction that Batman gives me.

It could be a film… or possibly a TV series you watched over and over again.

You may have fallen in love with the story and characters from a novel, and get a quiver of happiness every time somebody mentions it. You vividly remember those long summer afternoons where you sat curled up with the book open on your lap, lost in the world it conjured up in your imagination.

Remaining connected to the things that shaped who you are as a child is vitally important if you want to stay young at heart.

Yes, it's embarrassing to sob with happiness while watching a comic book movie, but I wouldn't trade that embarrassment for losing my attachment to the joys of my youth for all the tea in China.

I will be a Batman fan for as long as I live and proud of it.

These youthful passions are the building blocks of our personality and character - as much of an influence on us as the people we share our lives with.

…that's why I get a bit worried when I see the crap that's churned out for young people these days.

I may complain about getting older, but I wouldn't want to be a child or a teenager now for love nor money.

Can you imagine forming an emotional attachment to that pale berk from Twilight or Justin Bieber?

Aarrgghh!

The bastards!
The utter bastards!

Imagine my delight when I procured three bottles of Jack Daniels for the price of two at Sydney's Kingsford Smith airport.

Further imagine my pleasure as the bored looking girl behind the duty free counter *assured* me that getting the booze home would be easy and I wouldn't have to worry about the Thai customs authorities.

Imagine my total *disgust* when I rock up to the security desk and my bright yellow duty free bag is whisked away from me.

'No riquids this big!' the officious looking suit with a pencil moustache snaps at me.

'But the woman in Sydney said it would be ok!' I wail and bemoan, trying my hardest not to relinquish the death grip I've got on the bag, as a tiny woman with a tight perm yanks it from my grasp, causing the bottles inside to clank together loudly.

The noise draws the attention of everyone around and the red hue of embarrassment starts its inexorable march across my face.

'Those are rules! You must give!' the suit orders, eyebrows knitting in suppressed fury.

I know I should just let this one go.

After all, I'm standing in the customs area of a nation well known for locking up westerners at the drop of a hat. But I'm very tired, quite cranky and feeling ever so slightly *imperial.*

This often happens when British people are presented with an irritation while abroad in exotic foreign climes. We used to own all these buggers at one point and don't take it kindly when they start pushing us around.

'Now look my good man,' I enunciate clearly, channelling every hundred year old stereotype from the British Empire I can think of. 'I purchased this alcohol with good faith and intend to retain it!'

It's a crying shame I'm not wearing a safari suit and pith helmet right about now…

'It illegal to bring riquid through that this big,' the customs man tries to explain. 'Penalty for doing so include large fine and go to prison!'

A muscular looking security guard, who bears a disturbing resemblance to martial arts star Tony Jaa steps forward. If you don't know who Tony Jaa is, look up his films on Google and try to watch a couple – your elbows will ache in sympathy.

For what I believe to be the first time in my life, common sense steps forward at the correct moment to save my narrow English arse.

I let go of the duty free bag, sending the tiny woman staggering back, and address pencil moustache. 'I shall be lodging a formal complaint about this, sir!'

Oh yes. That should do the trick.

There's nothing guaranteed to get me reimbursed for the thirty dollars I've spent than an email fired off to the Bangkok airport authorities... CC'ed into the Foreign Office and Daily Mail.

So here I sit - on the same uncomfortable airport lounge seats - three bottle of Jack Daniels lighter, but very happy not to have been carted off for a full body cavity search - with a subsequent stretch in a Thai prison that someone would have to make a movie of the week about after my death.

Luckily, there don't appear to be any nose picking children or German sexual predators nearby this time around.

There aren't many people on the connecting flight back to the UK at all, it seems.

The fact that the flight over was jammed solid and the flight back is half empty probably speaks volumes about how popular Britain is these days...

Blimey, I've really been down on my country of birth in this book haven't I?

Sorry about that, it's just that there's so much about it these days that annoys me.

It gets my goat that our reputation throughout the world has been so tarnished in the past few years. I'm sick of not being able to feel any pride about the place.

We've lost our way in Britain and need to find it again.

Get that 'Great' bit back at the front.

...quite how this is to be accomplished is beyond me, but then I never claimed to be an expert on social reform.

I ranted and raved earlier about how all sense of personal responsibility has been taken away from us. I think having it re-established would be a good first step.

Then we probably need to imprison Simon Cowell in the Tower of London, next to the cell we've chucked Katie Price in. Tony Blair should be in the next one along and the editors of every tabloid newspaper can be crammed into the smallest cell at the end. They'll fit, don't worry. There probably won't be any room to breathe… but that would solve the problem once and for all wouldn't it?

Despite my dissatisfaction about the UK, I'm not going to lie to you – I'm still looking forward to touching down back on English soil.

We may be up shit creek without an economy right now, but there's always a resolve to the British people that remains indomitable.

The Dunkirk Spirit.

It's a cliché… but that doesn't mean it isn't true.

As a nation we have a never ending capacity to laugh in the face of adversity.

We'll also complain like *bastards* about it, but there will always be a certain amount of laughter going on as well.

War, economic disaster, health and safety gone mad, corrupt politicians, terrible weather… no matter what it is, you can bet the great British public will still be making jokes down the local pub and retaining the legendary stiff upper lip.

Apart from the petrol prices.

They're not fucking funny in the slightest…

7.29pm GMT (Yes, I'm just as confused as you are)
40386 Words
Over Burma. Or Myanmar, depending on how progressive you're feeling.

Yawn.

Back on the plane now and the hum of the engines is lulling me into a doze.

Am I supposed to be tired now?

According to my recently adjusted watch it's only 7.30pm. But at the same time it's also the middle of the night *and* early in the morning, depending on which perspective and time zone you want to look at it from.

It's at times like this I wish I had stronger drugs to choose from.

The caffeine is keeping me just about awake enough to write, but I'll be pissing like a racehorse if I keep drinking this much coffee for the next few hours.

Mind you, I wouldn't want to attempt writing while under the influence of harder narcotics.

I'd probably get about three coherent sentences written before just repeating the word 'thwibble' over and over again in increasingly large font sizes.

I guess that book might stand a chance of winning the Booker Prize - they'll award it to any old crap these days - but the likelihood of getting many sales on Amazon would be slim.

Drugs and I never had what you'd call a *happy* relationship.

My illegal narcotics taking days were exclusively between the ages of 18 and 21. I hadn't touched a drug before and haven't touched one since.

To be honest, I think I was just going through the motions half the time anyway, because doing drugs at the weekend was the done thing when you were a young, thrusting man in your late teens and early twenties.

Peer pressure managed to keep me on the 'gear' for about three years, before I kicked it to the kerb due to an increased sense of individuality and the desire to stop looking like an absolute tool every time I went clubbing.

…not wanting a criminal record in my early twenties was instrumental in giving drugs up too.

I say 'drugs' like I was some kind of hardcore narcotics fiend, but in truth I only ever dabbled in two or three over the course of those three years – restricting myself to cannabis, a couple of acid trips and one memorable, unpleasant occasion when I inadvertently smoked cocaine in a spliff at a Beastie Boys gig.

I remember getting a headache and sweating a lot, though the watered down lager and over enthusiastic PA system may have been equally responsible.

It was the second of my two sojourns into the wonderful world of LSD that put a stop to my drug taking days for good and all.

A couple of weeks after my twenty first birthday, I met up with some old friends I hadn't seen for ages.

I tended to socialise with people from university at that time, and the guys I'd hung around with in my teens had all gone their separate ways into jobs and education in cities all around the country.

Thinking back on it, this shindig was probably a last ditch attempt to relive the fun we'd had before adulthood got in the way. We were all determined to make it a night to remember!

It was a lovely Spring day – the country was undergoing a rather unexpected heat wave at the time – so we decided to visit the beer gardens of two local watering holes, before returning to my mate Big Kev's house to continue the party. His was the nearest to the town centre, had a decent sized garden and his mum and dad were away on holiday, so it was perfect.

Kev didn't live there anymore. He was at university in London, but had come home for the summer - returning briefly to the bosom of safety provided by the parental units.

There were ten of us in total. Seven lads and three girls.

This is a good ratio for a night out.

The presence of women mitigates the chances of the evening degenerating into a horrific drunken lout fest - and the chances of pulling always increase if you're out with girls already.

I've never understood why. In theory you'd think potential love interests would be put off by the presence of other women around you, but the reverse seems to be the case in practise.

This is probably one of those 'men are from Mars, women aren't fucking idiots' things I'll never get the hang of.

The first part of the evening went splendidly.

The warm sun bathed me in its soft radiance as I got nicely drunk on Heineken in the packed beer garden.

This was still a time when I thought excessive drinking came with no consequences. It would be more than a year before that belief was soundly proved to be inaccurate - as detailed in another anecdote elsewhere.

It was *so* nice in the beer garden that we never got to the second pub on our list.

Half eleven arrived and the bar started to empty, so we reluctantly left our temporary encampment and walked back to Kev's house.

This took a while, as what's the point in rushing when it's a balmy evening and you've already downed seven pints, eh?

A guy in our group called Liam - a mischievous lad of small dimensions I had nicknamed Goblin - thought it would be hilarious to jump inside a wheelie bin.

I completely agreed with this piece of comedy genius and happily pulled him down the road for a good two hundred yards before he said he felt sick and we had to stop so I could let him out.

There's the difference between being eighteen and twenty one...

Three years earlier I wouldn't have let him out until he *was* sick.

Once we all got back to Kev's, we cranked up the music, opened the twenty four pack of warm lager and toasted in the new day.

That was when Goblin said he'd scored some acid.

He'd always been the keenest on drugs out of the lot of us.

His teenage bedroom had been a shrine to all things marijuana related: Bob Marley poster, purple plastic bong, bean bag, smell of incense, take away menus – you know the kind of thing.

He was always the one out of his mind on amphetamine or LSD by the time the designated driver took us home from the nightclub.

There was one particularly memorable occasion when Clive The Scots Twat wouldn't give Goblin a lift home because he wouldn't stop humping the bonnet of Clive's F reg Golf.

Goblin had only six trips this evening, which could have been problematic as there were ten of us. Only four expressed an interest in taking one though, so there was more than enough to go around.

I was reluctant (to say the least) about being one of them, as I'd only ever done one acid trip before in my life.

Unfortunately, I'd also downed a healthy nine pints of beer so far that evening, which for a skinny bloke like me was a lot.

Drunkenness equals a complete inability to stave off peer pressure, so I caved in and took the fifth.

...and in any case, this was likely to be the last time this group of friends would be together, so why not kick the tyres and light the fires properly for a last big blow out? The wind was strong and caution was lobbed at it with no regard for personal safety.

If you're unfamiliar with acid trips - good for you - they come on sheets of paper with the drug impregnated into it, cut into perforated squares, each one counting as an individual 'trip'.

These squares usually have a picture printed on them - by way of some kind of half-arsed branding carried out by the manufacturers.

The cheery face of Fred Flintstone was on the ones Goblin produced.

Quite why I have no idea.

What a Hanna Barbera cartoon about prehistoric people has to do with hallucinogenic drugs is beyond me.

Maybe Hanna - and indeed Barbera - were off their collective tits when they dreamt the series up. Having watched the odd episode or two over the years I can well believe it. You'd have to be tripping your nuts off to think using a baby elephant to wash your dishes was a good idea.

The five off us - including Kev and Goblin - put the square tabs on our tongues and let the LSD drift into our bloodstreams.

I'm not going to deny I wasn't nervous.

Even through the alcoholic haze I knew I'd just dropped acid and would be 'coming up' in the next hour or so.

The last trip I'd experienced wasn't horrendous, but I could still remember getting quite freaked out when the street lights left mile long streaks of light in the sky as I stared at them from the passenger seat of Goblin's car.

An hour passes and *things* start to happen.

Trying to describe what you see during an acid trip can be very difficult, but the first half an hour or so went something like this:

Faces start to blur. Bodies start to change. The bulb in the lampshade overhead gets brighter and takes on a blue corona that shifts and pulses with every movement of your head. You sense that you're floating a couple of inches above your chair. Sounds take on a clipped, bright edge. Voices sound tinny. Music gets deeper. Angles warp. The world flattens. Every thought you have feels important. Every word you utter feels like it's the absolute truth. The images coming from the TV in the corner bleed into the room. If they ever invent holographic television, it'll look like this. You feel a drowsy sense of well being and a desire to just let yourself driiiiiiiiiiiift...

...

Then, I decided I was a banana.

One minute I'm grooving along to the Massive Attack pumping from Kev's stereo system, slowly waving my hands up and down in front of my face and giggling, the next I'm convinced I'm a long yellow fruit.

The switch is not gradual.

One second: Nick Spalding. The next: banana.

One second: human being. The next: the fruit of the genus *Musa* (gawd bless yer, Wikipedia).

The reason? I'd eaten a banana at lunch time.

I'd like to regale you with a funnier, less prosaic reason than that, but I like to keep things as truthful as the lawyers will allow.

This all sounds like the mother of all LSD related clichés, but it really did happen.

Explaining how I thought I was a banana is even harder than describing the more common effects of an acid trip, but I'll give it a bloody good go:

The world outside my bananery state is normal. The weird light effects have disappeared, the faces have ceased to blur and the sense of well being is gone. After all, a banana can't suffer from hallucinations can it? Being a banana is neither pleasant, nor unpleasant. You're just a banana. When I look down I still see my body, but I know deep down that it's just a disguise and that under my clothes I'm yellow with a Fyffes sticker on my chest. There is no doubt in my mind I am a banana. A special banana, I'll grant you – capable of sentient thought - but a banana nonetheless. I think of my banana cousin who I'd wickedly consumed earlier that day and feel a pang of self loathing and remorse. I am a traitor to banana-kind. I am the death of bananas. Luckily no-one in this room with me knows that. It's incredible. Here I am a banana in the company of human beings and none of them realise! None of them comprehend they are sitting in the room with a giant human-sized banana! I must tell them!

'I'm a banana.'

This is too quiet for any of the humans to hear over Massive Attack.

'I'm a banana!' I say louder.

'You what?' Melissa, the only girl to drop a Flintstone asks from the couch next to me.

'I'm a banana, Melissa.'

'You're a banana?' she says incredulously. The acid hasn't affected her as much, otherwise she might be telling me she was an orange and that we should jump in the nearest fruit bowl together.

'Yes. A banana.'

Melissa looks at Kev. 'Kev! Spalding thinks he's a banana!'

Kev – who'd been involved in a tense game of thumb wars with Carrie, the girl he'd been trying to penetrate for three unsuccessful years – looks round at me.

'Spalding? What's she on about?'

'Oh… oh, I'm a banana Kevin.' A polite banana it transpires, as this was the first time I'd ever addressed him by his full name.

Kev, a man full of alcohol and narcotics, starts to laugh.

This laughing fit will continue for the following three hours and will render him unable to take any further part in this anecdote.

Goblin, who's more used to this type of thing, senses an opportunity for some shenanigans. He comes over and squats on the arm of the sofa.

'You're a banana are you Spalding?' he says very seriously.

'Yes,' I reply, just as seriously.

'Are you ripe?' He's trying to keep a straight face, as are seven of the other people in the room. Kev's on the floor holding his stomach.

'Yes. I'm ripe and juicy.'

This sends Melissa off into a gale of laughter and makes poor old Kev nearly prolapse.

'Juicy, eh?' continues the evil Goblin. 'Do you... do you want somebody to eat you?'

Fabulous idea, Goblin. *Fabulous* idea.

'Eat me,' I pronounce in clipped tones.

'Eat me, eat me, eat me,' I repeat in quick succession in a strangled voice.

Until now I haven't mentioned Vanessa, the third in the trio of girls who have accompanied us on this bender.

Vanessa is a 'larger framed' lass and a Goth. Not the best of combinations, it has to be said.

While she's always been a nice person, Vanessa has developed a reputation over the years for being a bit of a misery guts. I've never seen her laugh out loud before. My banana impression changes this.

Vanessa (who I'll confess I used to call 'Van' in a rather obvious insult) lets out a bray of drunken laughter and throws her head in her hands, her portly frame shaking and threatening to burst from the black cobweb design sequined top she's wearing.

This in turn makes Kev laugh so hard it looks like somebody's electrocuting him.

...you'll notice that despite being as high as a kite, I'm still compos mentis enough to notice all these little details. The LSD has decided to fully focus on convincing me I'm a banana, leaving my faculties otherwise hideously intact and able to monitor the overall situation with disturbing accuracy.

Goblin leans forward. 'But you're a banana, Spalding. We can't just eat you like you are. That's not how you eat bananas...'

He's absolutely right! How stupid I've been! You have to peel a banana to eat it.

'PEEL ME!' I scream.

Kev throws up.

'PEEL ME!'

Melissa stuffs her face in a cushion.

'PEEL ME!'

Van's ample left breast pops out of her top.

'PEEEEEL MEEEE!'

Everyone else in the room starts to fall about the place in absolute hysterics as I order them to remove my peel in a high-pitched screech.

Even Goblin can't cope anymore. He's fallen off the arm of the sofa and is spread-eagled over the coffee table.

Well… if nobody's going to peel me, I'll just have to do it *myself*!

Off comes the jumper, swiftly followed by the Fruit Of The Loom t-shirt.

I'm unbuckling my belt – while still sat down I might add - when Melissa notice what I'm doing and tries to take steps.

'Nick! Nick! Stop it! You're not a banana!' she shouts, trying to hold my arms down.

'Yes. **YES I AM!**'

And you can't stop me fulfilling my bananery destiny, woman!

I lurch to my feet and pull down my jeans, exposing my boxer shorts – Batman ones. I can't get the jeans off completely though as I'm wearing a pair of enormous biker boots.

Bananas don't have legs and are therefore not particularly well co-ordinated when they discover they've apparently grown a pair.

I tumble over Goblin's distressed form and kick Kev in the head. He's too far gone to notice.

All this exertion has made me sweat a lot.

Combine that with the effect of the LSD on my body chemistry and I suddenly come over very warm and unpleasantly sweaty.

Bananas may come from hot countries, but this one is feeling decidedly uncomfortable in the fuzzy gloom of the lounge.

Egress is what's required to make me feel better, so I hop over to the kitchen and the back door beyond, which leads to the cool paradise of the garden.

Sadly this takes me past the kitchen table, on which is a fruit bowl.

Guess what fruit is in it…

My cousins! My banana brethren!

I can make up for my evil banana eating crimes by saving them from the same fate!

I gather up the bunch and clutch them to my chest.

Melissa has followed me out and attempts to wrangle them from my grasp.

'LEAVE THEM ALONE, BITCH!' I holler in an unholy rage and hop towards the door, banging it open with my hip. The cool fresh air is wonderful on my face, despite the fact I'm a banana and don't have one.

As an upstanding honourable banana who's read too much Batman, I know what must be done.

My poor banana friends must be set free. Released into the wild to frolic and gambol with no fear of being masticated by cruel humans!

I chuck the bunch of bananas into the garden as hard as I can. They describe a perfect arc in the moonlight... and go straight through the flimsy plastic garden shed window.

...Kev discovered them four days later rotting gently between the lawnmower and hose. The shed stunk of banana for several weeks I'm led to believe.

All of this is a bit too much for my banana brain to cope with and I collapse onto the grass - my face mashed into the soft earth, my arms splayed out to the sides like a fruity Jesus, and my arse stuck in the air, the Bat signal on display to any birds and low flying aircraft that might be passing.

There I remained for quite some time.

I know this because for the following few days I walked round with horrible aching legs from being stuck in one position for too long.

I stopped thinking I was a banana at about 5am as the effects of the LSD died away.

As I lay on the dew soaked grass, with the new sun bathing the world in its dawn glow, I reflected that hallucinogens and I should probably part company before something seriously unfortunate happened.

What if next time instead of thinking I was a banana, I decided I was a flying squirrel and chucked myself off the nearest tall building?

...small aside here: We've all heard stories of people dying in these circumstances, which begs the question: if you think you can fly when you're on drugs, why not try to take off from the *ground* instead of throwing yourself off the local multi-storey car park? You know... *just in case*?

With a furry tongue and wet arse I stumbled back into the house in the dawn's early light.

Everyone appeared to have gone home except Goblin, who lay fast asleep on the couch.

In petty retribution for making me think I was a banana, I found a permanent marker pen in the kitchen and wrote 'COCK' across his slumbering forehead.

This seemed like a proportionate response.

Since that night I've smoked one spliff at university – and that's it. No more illegal drugs have passed my lips.

…who's a good boy then?

Being a volunteer copper helped of course.

Floating into the parade room off your face on skunk isn't likely to win you any commendations.

You'll notice I'm making no moral judgements about drug taking.

It'd be a bit hypocritical of me to start lecturing about the dangers of drugs when I've spent a good portion of this book whinging that people have had their sense of personal responsibility taken away.

The dangers of drugs are there for all to see and I'm not going to repeat them here.

All I've done is outline my experience with illegal narcotics and why I haven't touched them in seventeen years.

But hey, if you want everyone to think you're a giant fruit and have the desire to spend the night lying on grass with your arse stuck in the air, then I'm sure one of the local dealers will be delighted to oblige you…

9.57pm GMT
43881 Words
Over China. I could murder a Kung Po Chicken.

Feels like we've been on this plane forever, doesn't it?

Much worse than the trip to Australia, because at least we had something to look forward to back then.

This flight is also a lot longer because we're going west.

I've never entirely understood why this should be the case. Maybe the wind blows harder that way?

Whatever the reason, we're still looking at over nine hours to kill before touchdown - which isn't a pleasant prospect, truth be told.

Praise the religious entity of your choice that we're up here in lovely Business Class, as opposed to all those poor folks down the back of the plane in Economy, who have to sit bolt upright for the whole flight.

Go on... stretch your toes out and have a big, comfortable yawn.

They won't see you doing it.

... probably just as well as you'd get lynched in about thirty seconds flat.

I'm going to put the laptop down and join you.

...

Lovely!

If you're going to get stuck on a plane for days, it's nice to have these little perks to relieve the stress, isn't it?

As you're no doubt aware by now, I'm the type of person that gets stressed quite easily.

There are many people like me.

Maybe you're one yourself.

Everyone suffers with stress to one extent or another, but everyone handles it in a different way.

Some cry, some drink, some get ulcers in their stomachs, some take weeks off work to the veiled disgust of their colleagues...

I shout at people.

It doesn't really matter who, as long as there's *somebody* standing within earshot to listen to Spalding's ranting.

I can't help it. I just get angry when I'm stressed and am a firm believer in externalising your emotions. It tends to prevent an ulcer from forming.

Having a good bellow is always a better way of dealing with anger than swallowing it down into a tight, hot ball that sits in the pit of your stomach and makes you unpleasant to be around at dinner parties.

The best way to externalise? Swearing.

Good old healthy, stress-relieving swearing.

Don't trust anyone who says swear words are bad and should never be uttered.

They're probably emotionally repressed psychopaths who will rip your throat out at any moment.

Swearing is fucking great and I highly encourage it.

Lay off it round you granny's house though. Nothing's likely to shuffle her off this mortal coil quicker than you screaming *'shit-eating donkey rapist!'* when your buttered scone falls on the floor.

Stress is directly related to your own personal circumstances of course.

Nobody gets all that stressed about the situation the Middle-East when they live in Chipping Sodbury, for instance.

Things have to be up close and personal if the stress demon is going to pay a visit and play havoc with your blood pressure.

You might have an important deadline at work.

You might be moving house.

You may have just found out your partner is cheating - or worse that they have a life threatening illness.

You may have just had you bank account cleaned out by fraudsters.

You may have just discovered your daughter is dating a notorious drug addict called Rapey Joe.

All these things can create a huge amount of stress and ruin your day.

…as can being dry humped by a chipmunk.

Let me explain:

For me, there are several environments that cause a lot of stress. They are - from least stressful to most - as follows:

My office.
The boss's office.
The dentist's waiting room.
France.
The M25 between 3 and 6pm.
Theme Parks.

Yes, you read the last one right… I hate theme parks.

Detest them.

Loathe them.

...I'm really, *really* not keen.

The reasons for this are threefold.

Firstly, I hate any form of forced jocularity.

Christmas is the chief offender, but right behind it are theme parks.

What gets my goat is that I'm essentially being told that whatever trials and tribulations I may be suffering in my life, the second I pass beyond the hallowed gates of the theme park, they will be disappear. I will become instantly *happy* and prepared to have a *really good time.*

No matter that I've just spent the best part of a month's wages to get into the bloody place - which automatically makes me *un*happy, and will be equally gouged by the prices of food, drink and merchandise while in there - further decreasing my general sense of well being.

Don't tell me what's fun and what isn't you stupid talking mouse, I'll make my own mind up!

Secondly, I hate children.

Yes, I do have a seven year old son, but as previously stated this doesn't mean I have to love all the other little bleeders out there, does it?

Far from it, in fact.

I'll put up with Tom erupting into a tantrum in the middle of McDonalds when I buy him the wrong Happy Meal because he's my kid, but I sure as shit wouldn't if it was somebody else's squalling brat rolling around on the floor covered in French fries.

If ever there were a true testament to the power of love it's that I can raise my son with care and compassion. If he wasn't mine I'd quite happily drop-kick the little fucker into the next county at the first given opportunity.

Children are the unholy denizens of theme parks.

Please don't kid yourself that these places are 'adult friendly'. This is marketing bollocks of the highest order.

Billions are spent every year convincing you that a day surrounded by brightly painted fibre-glass, high-pitched music piped at you over a loud tannoy, and extremely long queues for extremely short rides is perfectly acceptable entertainment for a fully grown adult.

Don't believe a word of it.

There's only one adult theme park in the world. It's called Las Vegas.

The day Disneyland offers a ride called the 'Vagina-rama' and serves German lager on tap I might reconsider this position.

Thirdly, theme parks are always a pain in the arse to get to, because they are *always* miles from your house. Even if you live next door to one.

Because who wants to visit a theme park that's just down the road, eh? That's not a proper *adventure.*

No, the theme park must be *at least* a three hour drive away.

You must awaken in the middle of the night and set off around dawn to avoid the traffic - which never works. Arrival at the theme park will involve twenty five minutes driving round looking for a parking space, followed by thirty five minutes queuing to get to the cash desk, where you will part with hundreds of pounds for the privilege of queuing for rides for a further four to five hours.

And if you're very lucky you'll be harassed for the entire day by a maniac dressed up as a giant chipmunk, to add to the 'fun'.

I'm in Florida with Sophie, a two year old Tom, my brother, his wife and their fat children – an eleven year old boy and a fourteen year old girl respectively.

My sister, knowing a fucking awful idea for a holiday when she hears one, has opted to go on a canal barge vacation in the Cotswolds with her husband. This shows a greater degree of common sense and foresight than either my brother Mike or I are able to summon.

Mike will never read this book, so I can cheerfully refer to his children as fat, because they are.

His wife is also fat.

He wouldn't mind me saying that either as she ran off with her boss in 2008.

Mike has since met a woman nine years his junior, so it all worked out for the best. Especially because he met her in a pub like a normal person and didn't (like me) have to meet the soup slurping French Gollum-a-like or Princess Menopause.

Mike's fat kids - whose names I shall not reveal here, but let's call them Augustus and Imelda for the comedy value – both fit in well with the inhabitants of Florida, as does his fat wife She-bitch.

…She-bitch is also not her real name, in case you were wondering.

Sophie is a size eight, my paunch is behaving itself and Tom is too small to worry about, so we certainly *don't* fit in with the human barrage balloons all queuing outside Disneyworld on this hot July morning in 2006.

The drive from the hotel we're staying in up the coast took exactly three hours and one minute, but parking was relatively easy, much to my surprise, and we only drove round for twenty one minutes looking for a space.

It's only nine in the morning and I'm already starting to get a tension headache.

This isn't helped by the muzak being piped down onto the queue at ear-bleeding volume.

Even this doesn't quite drown out the mewling cries of a selection of fat American children, who are all desperate to get wedged into the seats of a slew of extremely short, brightly coloured rides for the next eight hours of their portly lives.

This would all be more bearable if people would just stop fucking smiling at me.

If it's possible to cause alarm, harassment and distress to an individual just by grinning at them, the staff of Disneyworld are experts at it. It probably requires years of extensive training.

Every single automaton employed by Disney effects a toothy grin that never reaches the eyes.

I light up a cigarette as we approach the ticket booth.

One of the toxic smilers picking up litter politely asks me to put it out.

I glare, but do as I'm told. I don't want to risk the wrath of the obese monsters crowding round me.

This is America after all, where people will sue at the drop of a hat. These elephants might eat the gross national product of The Sudan every day, but god forbid they breathe in any cigarette smoke and damage their blubber covered lungs.

We pay at the till and Augustus lets out a squeal of piggy delight as he negotiates his fat arse through the turnstile, swiftly (ha!) followed by Imelda and her enormous Three Musketeers chocolate bar.

She-bitch waddles in after them, bouncing off her fellow behemoths as everyone funnels towards 'the happiest place on earth' and the nearest all-you-can-fucking-hoover-up buffet.

An aside: You may be detecting a dislike of fat people here.

It's subtle, but if you re-read the above paragraphs you might just pick up on it.

Don't get me wrong, standard chubsters are ok. I've got nothing against people who may be carrying a few extra pounds. After all, with today's stressful work-oriented lifestyle, having the time to take regular exercise and eat well can be a problem. I myself have a bit of a gut because of it.

What I *don't* have is thighs that audibly rub together when I walk.

I can also stroll a hundred yards without breaking into a sweat, think eating six hot dogs at once is excessive, and don't watch Supersize Vs Superskinny wondering what all the fuss is about.

There is *no* justification for looking like a walrus that's been rolled through Primark. None at all.

And don't give me the old 'I had a hard childhood' excuse either. I'm pretty sure Anne Frank's was worse and she didn't need a reinforced toilet seat in her attic, did she?

Anyway…

I trudge after the rest of my family like a man going to the gallows.

Sophie is in a mood with me because I've had a face like thunder for the past two hours.

'Can't you just *try* to enjoy yourself?' she asks.

'Surely if you have to make an effort to enjoy yourself, the chances are you're not doing something particularly enjoyable?' I counter, earning a scowl.

I let her and Tom speed up to join She-bitch and Mike, and I spark up another cigarette.

This is when the giant chipmunk assaults me for the first time. A seven foot rodent with googly eyes and the most gormless expression I've ever seen in my life.

It could have approached one of the myriad fat children as they waddled towards the first concession stand. They can't move very fast, so even a Disney staff member in a huge chipmunk costume should be able to catch one of the colossal buggers before it gets away. Instead though, it decides to target the grumpy thirty three year old man smoking a Marlboro.

Over it waddles, arms outstretched in the universal signal for 'hug'.

Now, I don't behave very well at this point. I'm hot, tired, stressed and not looking forward to this day from Hell one iota. I don't treat the situation well.

'Fuck off,' I tell the chipmunk.

It stops in its tracks.

Even through the layers of thick material and plastic I can tell the person inside is shocked and appalled at the use of such hideous language in the happiest place on earth.

The chipmunk puts one hand on its hip, cocks its oversized head to one side and waggles an admonishing finger at me.

Well, this is just marvellous. I'm now being chastised by a giant chipmunk for the use of the F-word.

'Sorry.'

…and now I'm apologising to the bloody thing.

If he/she/it had left it there, the rest of my day might not have been quite so bad.

However, rather than just turning away and chasing down one of the lard balls, the chipmunk decides my apology isn't quite good enough and decides to hug the hate out of me.

It strides forward, arms outstretched again, this time at such a speed I'm unable to avoid it.

I find myself enveloped in rough fur - my cigarette crushed on the side of its hard head.

The chipmunk's grip is vice-like and it starts to shake me in what it probably thinks is a gesture of happy camaraderie. I just feel like I'm being molested.

I've only been in this bloody place for a few minutes and I'm already being sexually violated by a woodland creature.

Augustus has noticed what's going on and squeals in delight, drawing the attention of the rest of my family unit. Sophie immediately takes a picture, the smile on her face so evil Genghis Kahn would have found it disturbing.

Other people have also noticed what's going on and are watching the entertainment unfold. A crowd is forming around me.

This is getting beyond a joke.

My molestation by a tree dwelling mammal has now become a spectator sport.

I push the chipmunk away as hard as I can without risking an assault charge.

The bastard inside the costume staggers back, gives me a long hard look and hangs its stupid big head.

I'm now the bad guy...

Fat, sticky children all around me start to boo. Seriously... they're *booing* me. Like I'm the villain in a third rate pantomime.

I feel the typical flush of embarrassment colour my cheeks and start to regret ever having agreed to come on this holiday.

Without saying a word to Sophie, Mike or She-bitch I march off towards Epcot, hoping to lose myself in the crowd and put this trying situation behind me.

That's the end of this story, right?

Wrong.

The chipmunk isn't finished with me yet.

I don't know who was inside, but whoever they were, they must have targeted me for special treatment.

I guess being dressed in a heavy, hot costume all day can get a bit tiresome, so if you can generate some fun to alleviate the monotony it's no bad thing. Chipmunk's decided *I'm* the fun for the rest of that particular day.

The bastard is hanging around the Magic Kingdom.

This is the area *we're* staying in for the whole day, of course.

Mike has come up with some kind of grand master plan for the three days we'll be subjected to this circle of Hades, and day one is all about spending time in the Magic Kingdom - which is laid out likes spokes on a wheel, with Cinderella's big ugly plastic castle at the hub.

To move through the various areas you have to pass the castle quite a lot and this is where my chipmunk nemesis has stationed itself for the day.

Three soul destroying hours after our first encounter, round two begins.

My family have spent the morning queuing for rides and eating anything in sight, while I've been wishing the Ebola virus was airborne and more communicable.

I've smoked like a trooper, my feet are killing me and I have a sunburnt forehead almost as bad as the one I'm sporting now thanks to the Australian sun.

It's lunchtime. Augustus and Imelda haven't eaten for at least six microseconds and the poor little blighters look like they're about to waste away, so we're in search of a decent place for them to trough - and for me to hopefully buy some quick, fast acting poison.

I'm completely oblivious to the attack before it comes.

One second I'm ambling along looking at the giant plastic castle and wishing I was dead, the next minute I'm being dry humped.

I swear to god, it's like a horny Great Dane has taken a shine to me.

I let out a cry of terror as the furry arms grab me from behind.

I never do see who is inside throughout this episode, but he must have been a big, strapping fucker with arms like steel.

I have no chance of breaking free as the chipmunk sexually assaults me once again, this time in full view of hundreds.

'Let me go!' I bleat inanely.

This has gone from annoying to vaguely disturbing.

'Please?'

My mewling tone strikes a chord and before things can go too far the chipmunk lets me go.

I stumble away and look back at it looming over me.

It puts both hands on its hips and effects a shoulder shaking laugh, googly eyes rolling around as it savours my humiliation.

Before I can register any complaint, the monster turns on one furry heel and makes its way back through the crowd, disappearing into the throng of human zeppelins - off to harass somebody else no doubt.

For the rest of the day I'm like a coiled spring - expecting ambush at every turn.

Any time one of the myriad costumed idiots approaches me, my guard goes up and I start looking for weak spots.

It's touch-and-go when Goofy homes into view - he's a tall bugger and I'm not taking any chances. Thankfully he just ruffles Tom's hair and I'm not forced to engage in hand-to-hand combat.

My stress levels are now so high it's a wonder my eyeballs don't pop out of my head.

Not only am I subjected to the abject misery of a boiling hot Florida day in a theme park, I have the added fun of furred sexual assault to worry about.

Come 6pm I'm considering the purchase of some weapons of mass destruction.

I figure there's probably an ex-pat Russian community in Florida somewhere and I should be able to track down at least one chemical weapon from the black market.

For the first time that day I'm feeling happy as I lean against a shady beech tree close to Liberty Square, contemplating at what location and time I should set the bomb off. Half past ten in the morning next to the statue of Walt and Mickey should yield a high enough casualty rate, all things considered.

Augustus and Imelda, having crashed massively from the insane sugar rush they've been on all day are flaked out on nearby bench.

She-bitch has fucked off to find a new SD memory card for her camera, leaving Mike the solace of a few minutes peace to think about the mistakes he's made in life.

Sophie looks rather adorable fanning herself with her sun hat and sipping a refreshing cold bottle of orange juice. Tom is fast asleep, the lucky little bugger.

As I smoke a cool cigarette in the blissful shade, chipmunks are the furthest thing from my mind.

And then I turn my head to the right.

There he is.

Cold, dead googly eyes staring at me…

Mammalian mouth turned up at the sides in a hideous broad grin…

Thick, matted paws held out, ready to grab me…

'Tis truly the stuff of nightmares.

I want to run. Honestly I do. But I'd never live it down. I'd never be able to look at my son again, the shame in his child's eyes too much to bear.

Instead, I do what any self respecting British person does in such circumstances - I look away and try to ignore it.

I stare fixedly towards the plastic castle, hoping chipmunk will give up and leave me be.

No such luck.

From the periphery of my vision I can see it approaching in a ridiculous mock stealth shuffle.

I continue to ignore it right until it's barely three foot away.

A moan escapes my lips as it throws its arms open again and waddles toward me.

With the tree to my back I have nowhere to go and the crushing, humiliating hug begins again.

I try to get away, but chipmunk is having none of it. It means to have me and there's nothing I can do to stop the costumed rapist.

The jiggling and shaking begin again, and I can feel its coarse fur scraping all over my defenceless body.

In a final desperate bid for freedom I jerk forward, knocking us both off balance.

Both chipmunk and I stagger past the tree... tripping up and disappearing over a conveniently placed row of bushes behind it.

Thankfully we've spun round in the struggle and I land on top of him, rather than the other way around. Being crushed to death by a chipmunk is a headline my family and friends would never live down.

I think at this point the bored staff member inside the costume realises he's gone *way* too far.

Springing up, the massive head flops around as the guy inside looks in all directions to see if anyone has seen this gross invasion of a customer's privacy.

'Yeah! Yeah, you'd better be worried, you bastard!' I exclaim with vengeful joy. 'I'm going to complain!'

I'm now shouting. 'Your superiors will hear about this!'

I point a finger of doom at the chipmunk.

...who flips me the bird.

Actually, properly, stabs one fuzzy chipmunk middle digit in the air and waggles it at me.

Then, like the slowest, brownest, furriest ninja you've ever seen, it's gone... running further into the carefully cultivated woodland area we fell into before I can give chase.

I am incredulous.

Nick Spalding is the only human being on Earth this kind of thing could happen to.

Nothing essentially *criminal* has taken place. No-one has been hurt and in the grand scheme of things being targeted by a mischievous Disney character isn't all that big a deal – but it *always happens to me*.

I only fill these bloody books with anecdotes like this as a coping mechanism, you know…

That was the lowlight of the holiday.

…one I'm constantly reminded of every time I go to Mike's house.

You see, Sophie printed off the photo she'd taken of me and chipmunk and gave it to Mike. He put it in a frame… and there it sits to this day on top of his piano.

A testament to my shame.

If you ever want to torture me, just chain me to a bench and put 'Chip 'n Dale Rescue Rangers' on the TV. Poke me with a sponge at the same time and I'll tell you anything.

3.41am GMT
47872 Words
Over Poland. I will resist any obvious plumbing jokes at this point.

Well, once again we're coming to the end of our time together.

It's been over forty hours - with a long break in the middle - since we settled in for the story about the Big Fucking Yellow Waders.

Tempus has once again fugited mightily…

We're speeding towards the shores of Britain and soon the words 'The End' will be writ large across the bottom of the page.

I have to say that writing this book has been a greater pleasure than the first.

This is partially due to the fact I've been able to take breaks and have been sat in a very comfy seat, but just as important is the fact I know I have an audience who actually likes reading this waffle.

The reaction to Life… With No Breaks was genuinely very humbling and made me feel quite proud of myself.

Every positive review, comment and opinion put a smile on my face and a warm glow in my heart.

While writing the book was an absolute nightmare, the subsequent interaction I've had with people on various internet forums has been highly enjoyable.

In that spirit, I thought the final chapter of this book could continue that interaction somewhat.

A few weeks ago I asked forum users to email me any questions they'd like to ask, on any subject they'd like me to talk about. What follows is my attempt to answer the pick of the bunch.

So if you don't like this section, you only have yourselves to blame:

Babyblues says:
When did you realise you were funny?

Funny ha-ha, or funny peculiar?

Assuming you mean the first option, the truthful answer is I have no idea.

I'm not even sure I *am* funny, when you get right down to it.

I suppose I have to believe it because people tell me I am… and I don't just mean my mother.

Also, I don't think I'm necessarily funny in real life, just on the page.

———

145

Don't corner me and ask me to tell you a joke, because it'll go very badly. I tend to either forget the punch line completely, get it wrong, or substitute it for one from a completely different gag.

There's a joke that goes:

What have Ayrton Senna and Michael Owen got in common?

Neither of them can take a corner.

Funny... if a little sick.

It's *not* funny at all when you say *Clive* Owen instead of Michael Owen.

The look of blank incomprehension as people try to consolidate the death of a Formula One driver with the bloke who isn't James Bond, but was in that flick where you nearly saw Natalie Portman's growler, is one for the books.

If you've read Life... With No Breaks you'll know I always wanted to be a writer from an early age, but it's only been in recent years that I've discovered the only thing I'm any good at writing is comedy, apparently.

How upsetting.

There I was, determined to write a scorching fantasy epic that'd make A Game Of Thrones look like The Hungry Caterpillar... when it turns out my talent is more geared towards wank gags and stories about being a banana.

Sigh.

Still, it's worked alright for Terry Pratchett - and if I could have a even a crumb sized portion of his success I'd be more than happy to be pigeonholed as a humorist.

...if you meant funny peculiar, it was in 1996 and I still haven't got over the shock.

Gingerlily says:

I think there's lots of mileage to be had from the strange things that happen to perfectly normal people when they get behind a keyboard and a pseudonym and start posting on forums...

It's a weird phenomenon isn't it?

The internet has effectively turned us all into really terrible superheroes.

We've got the alter-ego, but instead of having the amazing special powers to go with it, all we have is the ability to criticise the acting in Sex And The City and argue about whether Gandalf would beat Dumbledore in a fight or not.

...my money's on Gambon if he's drunk enough.

The keyboard and screen offer a fantastic buffer between us and the rest of the world. A psychological suit of armour we don before going into battle with the trolls.

The internet spreads freedom of speech across the globe - and it's never easier to speak freer than when no bastard knows who you really are.

Kevin Peebles may be a acne ridden seventeen year old virgin living in Dagenham, with a squint and questionable bathroom habits in real life - but you'd better not cross verbal swords with his online alter-ego 'Da_Sex_Captain_94' if you want to escape with your hide intact.

The media - and beardy intellectual types who make a living commentating on society - tend to think folks like this are quite the inferior bunch. They're meant to be objects of scorn – sat all alone in their bedrooms, living a soulless hollow existence in a mindless digital landscape.

Bull testicles, I say…

If a shy reclusive type - who would otherwise be too afraid to raise a voice - feels empowered to rant about overuse of CGI in modern cinema using a pseudonym, then more fucking power to them I say.

…and maybe - just maybe - that shy reclusive type isn't Kevin Peebles in Dagenham.

Instead let's say *her* name is Adiba, and she lives in a country famous for its religious oppression, crackdowns on free speech and torture of civilians.

I'll happily put up with ten million idiots hiding behind a silly username to moan about how Spiderman's new costume looks shit, if it also means somebody like Adiba can hide behind an alter-ego and let the world know the truth about the terrible things happening in her country.

Free speech is a double-edged sword, but I'd like to think the positive edge is sharper.

For my part, I've struggled somewhat with the glorious internet revolution and social networking phenomenon, but am slowly getting there…

The line about shutting down the Japanese National Grid in the last book still holds true, but if you want to be a writer these days, having a decent working knowledge of the blogosphere (see? I know all the terminology) and social networking is a must.

More and more of us are deciding on what we want to waste our valuable free time doing based on the things we see online.

You can't promote your wares these days - whatever they may be - without an effective web presence.

A book is as much a product as anything, so I've had to get used to online networking pretty damn quickly.

This has led to many sleepless nights trying my hardest to work out HTML - usually in the pursuit of a swanky looking signature to go below the posts I make on forum message boards, in the desperate hope somebody will click on the link and buy my book.

Incidentally: **Life... With No Breaks** is still available!
...ahem.

Fiona McFee says:
Why are there no vampires in Life... With No Breaks? And which would you prefer to be - a vampire or a werewolf?

Funny you should bring this up.

I did have a go at writing a book capturing the current zeitgeist of paranormal shenanigans recently. They're selling like hot cakes and I thought I should hitch a ride on the bandwagon.

After all, these non-fiction chuckle-fests are fun, but I'm not likely to be buying a mansion and a yacht off the back of them any time soon, am I?

I started with the best of intentions, but things fell apart rapidly.

I was brought up on Hammer horror films, so the idea of making a vampire or a werewolf the romantic hero of the story felt *utterly* wrong.

I tried.

I really did.

But every time I manufactured a scenario where the heroic floppy-haired vampire goes to save the life of the beautiful but troubled heroine... he ends up biting her head off and bathing in her blood instead.

I'm sorry, but that's what vampires *do*, isn't it?

Call me old fashioned if you like, but mincing around wearing eye shadow and twinkling whenever the sun comes out doesn't sound like the kind of person who'd be a direct descendent of Vlad The Impaler, does it?

Perhaps they shouldn't be called vampires...

'Toothypoofs' sounds more accurate.

If ever you needed proof that vampires weren't real, look no further than the fact Stephenie Meyer and Robert Pattinson are still alive.

Any self respecting creature of the night would have slaughtered those two a long time ago for bringing their kind into such disrepute.

It's like writing a book about neo-Nazis where you have them flounce around in pink frilly knickers, man-kissing and baking fairy cakes. Chances are you're going to get a metal swastika shoved up your arse before you can say New York Times Best Seller.

There are no vampires – or toothypoofs - in Life... With No Breaks because I've never met one.

...unless you count the old woman in Beverly Hills. I can well believe she's lived for thousands of years and sucks the life out of everyone around her.

I would prefer to be vampire myself, for the pure and simple reason they get to fuck more.

It might be groovy to transform into a wolf and go prowling the city streets at night, but hairy palms and dog breath aren't likely to get you into the knickers of the local good time girls, are they?

Also, I used to be into heavy metal so am well used to wearing black clothing.

We never went in for the eye-liner thing back in my day though. Much more macho back in the eighties... if you can call a penchant for denim and long greasy hair macho, that is.

I suppose the reason for the continued popularity of vampires is that they get to have lots of sex. Even the drippy ones who twinkle majestically when they go out into the sunlight - rather than bursting into flames, screaming at the top of their lungs, as is right and proper.

The fantasy of living forever, staying eternally young... and getting to penetrate as many young women as possible is undeniably attractive.

Attractive to *men* anyway.

I don't understand the female mind (naturally), but I suppose there must be something sexually alluring about a man who can carry off a black cloak and vague Eastern European accent with aplomb.

Personally, I've always preferred zombies.

I'm sure this probably says something hideous about my character, but it's getting way too close to the end of the flight now for any kind of introspective analysis - which is probably just as well for both our sakes.

Zombies rock, let's just leave it at that, shall we?

Millertron says:
Is the stuff you write true, or are you actually full of shit?

You're not the only person to ask me this.

And who can blame you? I barely believe some of the ridiculous things that have happened to me - and I was there, so I should know.

They are all true though – even if I've described them in a way designed to maximise the laughs - you'll forgive me that, won't you?

I've said it before, but I'll say it again, I firmly believe *anyone* could write anecdotes from their past that would be as funny - if not funnier - than the stuff I've been through.

Sceptics suggest that no one person could have all these horrible things happen to them, unless their name was Basil Fawlty.

I always come back with the argument that they certainly *can* happen to one person - and the only difference between me and everyone else is that I'm a humour writer with a faulty censorship switch and a disturbingly good memory...

6.09am GMT
49885 Words
Over the English Channel. I *really* need to get off this plane now...

Cue the Dam Busters theme...the music from The Great Escape... Rule Britannia sung by a heavenly choir... and Jerusalem belted out by a couple of hundred fat Welshmen in tuxedos.

Yes, we're just about to fly into UK airspace and if you look out of your window you'll notice that – *gasp* – it looks like it's going to be a sunny day!

Nothing like the hammering Sydney heat we left what seems like a lifetime ago, but a mild, calm day in England's green and pleasant land nevertheless.

It's enough to put a smile on your face and a spring in your step.

The prospect of finally getting out of this long metal tube also fills me with delight.

I'm entirely sick of the low hum of the Rolls Royce engines and the sure knowledge I've been breathing other people's farts for an entire day, thanks to the way the air conditioning system works.

What started off as a very comfortable seat has now turned into a medieval torture device.

My legs are restless, my tongue is furry and I'm sure a spot has appeared on my forehead that wasn't there when we boarded in Australia.

Who says air travel is a drag, eh?

Looks like you've faired better than me.

I can see your left leg twitching a bit, but your skin hasn't taken on that pallid look people get when they've been in the air a long time and there are no new visible spots or blemishes that I can see.

Well done! You must be getting your five a day.

As we start the descent into Heathrow I'd just like to once again say thank you very much for accompanying me on this journey.

This will sound *very* corny, but I wouldn't have written this book without knowing you'd be a part of it again.

Stephen King calls his audience 'constant readers', which has a nice ring to it. I tend to prefer the phrase 'constant listeners' as it fits better with my style.

...hark at me, eh?

I knock out two observational comedy books and think I have a right to compare myself to one of the most popular authors in history.

I think I'm a little light-headed from jet lag.

Time to put your seat belt on… the captain's just ordered us to through his moustache.

I hope you enjoyed this second trip through the deformed wasteland of my subconscious and that there a few nuggets of dubious wisdom you can take from it.

As ever, the most important thing is that it made you chuckle… spiriting you away for a couple of hours from this gloomy recession hit world, where the laughs are in short supply these days.

I'm now going to turn the laptop off and look forward to the landing, which I hope will be smooth.

Then all I have to do is get through customs looking like a burns victim, pick up my overflowing suitcase and find my (hopefully non-vandalised) BMW in the car park.

If I ever write a third one of these I'll tell you how it went…

All the best,
Nick.

The End

6.41am GMT
50421 Words
At the end of the road

About the author:

Nick Spalding is an author who, try as he might, can't seem to write anything serious. He's worked in the communications industry his entire life, mainly in media and marketing. As talking rubbish for a living can get tiresome (for anyone other than a politician), he thought he'd have a crack at writing comedy fiction - with an agreeable level of success so far, it has to be said. Nick lives in the South of England with his fiancée. He is approaching his forties with the kind of dread usually associated with a trip to the gallows, suffers from the occasional bout of insomnia, and still thinks Batman is cool.

Nick Spalding is one of the top ten bestselling authors in eBook format in 2012.

You can find out more about Nick by following him on Twitter or by reading his blog Spalding's Racket.

Printed in Great Britain
by Amazon